G000060009

Other books in the Sunny Cove Series

Makeup and Mayhem

Eyebrows and Evil Looks

Nails and Nightmare

A

Sunny Cove

COZY MYSTERY

Book One

1

Selling makeup is easy when your client is desperate. This desperation might be due to an impending landmark event, a desire to impress or simply the need to replenish an exhausted supply. Either way, the exchange of cash for goods is much quicker when the common denominator of desperation is in play. Celia Dube was a master at discerning the varied manifestations of this desperation and was equally adept at offering the solution. She had been a beauty consultant and makeup distributor in the Cape Town suburb of Oasis Bay for the last twelve years.

As Celia watched her older son running around the kitchen that morning, she was glad she didn't have the pressure that a nine-to-five job brought to a large percentage of the working population.

"You can't wear the Superman cape to school today!" Celia said to her nine-year-old son James, who was giggling as he ran rings around the kitchen island, his arms stretched in front of him like a superhero cutting through the air at thirty-five thousand feet. She timed his run and swooped him up into her arms. As James wriggled playfully, Celia undid the cape strap around his neck and took it off. She placed him back on the floor and straightened his slightly ruffled school shirt.

"So when will I wear it?" James asked. He was a charmer, with tiny beady eyes and dimples when he smiled that she often found disarming.

"We'll do that over the weekend at the beach, okay, sweetie?" Celia replied. "Go get your brother away from the TV so we can leave," she added, satisfied that he was fully dressed up.

Celia watched James run into the living room that was painted with the orange rays of morning sunlight. His younger brother John was engrossed with his favorite cartoon, all smiles and focus. So caught up was he that when James called out his name, John didn't even flinch.

Celia reached for the remote control atop the kitchen island, which she kept close for moments like these, and switched the television off.

"Oh, Mom! It was almost finished!" John spun around to look at his mother, wearing his best version of a frown. The boys were pretty good actors, Celia always observed.

"No, it wasn't baby. Come on, we're running late for school. You will catch up in the evening, okay?"

"Promise?" John asked with puppy eyes.

"I promise," Celia replied, with one hand over her heart. John's wide smile returned. Now bounding with energy, John ran towards the front door.

"Come get your backpacks first!" Celia said as she reached for two little backpacks placed on the kitchen stools: a rugged, small khaki one for James and a new blue one for John. Her husband Trevor, a hulk of a man who served in the military, had used the khaki bag to carry daily essentials during one of his military missions in East Africa. When Trevor left it behind as he went on his last tour of duty, James had claimed it and made it his school bag, discarding the new bag she had bought him.

It had been five years, and the khaki bag had seen better days, but James would never think of getting another one. Celia didn't even want James to change it because she loved the memories of Trevor that it brought back.

John got to his backpack first, grabbing it just as James arrived. It had become a competition, as it always was with boys.

"Be careful!" she said for the umpteenth time that

morning.

James slung his backpack faster than his younger brother and pretended it was now a jetpack, resuming his 'fly-through-the-air' antics to get to the door first. He opened the door, and John walked through it before James could squeeze past. Amused, Celia quickly grabbed an apple from the fruit bowl, as well as her car keys, and followed them out.

They emerged into a sunny Cape Town morning as the sun peered out through the tall trees surrounding their home. She loved the fact that they were in the suburbs, away from the skyscrapers and the concrete of the city center. When Trevor had suggested making their family home in the suburbs, she had jumped at it. Though they had good times in the big city, coming back home to the close-knit community she was familiar with was her dream for raising a family. With time, she had fallen totally in love with the practicality of it all. Here, they could take walks when needed and the boys had plenty of room to play as they explored the landscape and enjoyed the sandy beaches. It wasn't called one of the most beautiful places in the world for nothing.

Celia unlocked the Subaru station wagon, and the boys jumped into the back seats.

"Seatbelts!" Celia said.

"Check!" the boys replied out of sync as they frantically hurried to belt up.

Celia was about to switch on the car when she realized she had forgotten the bag of beauty products in the house. They were crucial to her daily run of driving around to meet clients, make deliveries and offer her expertise as a beauty consultant.

"Oh, drat," she whispered under her breath.

"Oh, drat!" James parroted back gleefully.

Celia turned back to look at him. His smile almost disarmed her again, but she needed to draw a line here.

"What did we say about talking back to mommy?"

"Don't talk back unless you ask us a question," James replied.

 "Good. Let's keep it that way, okay?" she said, smiling. James nodded. Celia hoped she wouldn't have to do that very often.

"All right guys, let's get back out."

"Why?" James asked.

"Mommy forgot her products in the house. Come on, I need a pair of strong hands," she said as she got out of the car.

The kids followed her to the house.
 A few years ago, Celia would have left the boys in the car–what harm would a thirty second wait do? A lot. Celia had once made them wait in the car as she went back for something she had forgotten. When she returned, she found a scruffy, strange man walking up to the car. She screamed her lungs out, and he took off. Trevor, who was home that morning, came out with a gun. Since then, they resolved to always keep the boys close, and Celia wasn't about to drop the ball on that one.

She got the bag of beauty products without much ado, and they walked back to the car. Celia rarely forgot things, and when she did, she knew it could be a sign of exhaustion. It had been an intense couple of weeks running the business and a whole household with two energetic boys. As she fought to keep her wits sharp, she wished Trevor was around to help her.

"What's drat, Mom?" James asked. They were at the front courtyard of the school.

"Well, in the evening, when you tell me all the good things that will happen in school today, I'll also tell you what that is. Deal?" Celia said. James nodded.

She hugged both of her sons and watched them walk up the steps and into the school building.

Celia headed back to the spot where she had parked her car and got in. Instead of driving off, she took a moment to do something that was becoming a habit: people watching. Looking on as parents dropped off their children, Celia narrowed her focus to the mothers.

Some women were office workers who needed to drop off their kids before embarking on the half-hour drive to the city center. Celia liked their trim outfits that suited the corporate office spaces they worked in. Some had office access tags hanging off their necks because they would only have seconds to race into their offices before their bosses raised hell. Savvy!

The other group appeared to be housewives. They were the ones who always had no urgency to their drop off routine; many would seek to do the final touches to their kids' uniforms while in the parking lot. They would also have separate lunch boxes for their kids and take the longest to say goodbye. Cute!

Watching both groups in action, Celia figured she was somewhere in the middle. She had the urgency and focus of the office-going women, and the motherly care and flexibility of the housewives.

She took out her notebook and looked through the list of client deliveries she needed to make. It was a day full of back-to-back deliveries, and she resolved that if it got too hectic, she would readjust her schedule and add an afternoon siesta to the mix.
First on the list was Christine Owens, a seventy-year-old feisty woman who lived close by. She had been a good client initially, but her enthusiasm for prompt payment had recently been replaced with an indifference that Celia didn't like. Celia didn't run her business on credit, but had made an exception with Mrs. Owens on her last delivery because she was a good family friend. Since then, it had been hard to get Mrs. Owens to pay up.

Maybe it was time for a change in approach.

The Macan Residences was a quiet, semi-posh residential neighborhood full of robust, identikit bungalows. A lot of older residents with a decent bit of money lived there, forming a crucial community of peers who supported each other as they lived through their sunset years. The relative affluence of the place made Celia wonder why Mrs. Owens wouldn't pay her dues.

Mrs. Owens' house was at the corner of the street. It had blue highlights to its cream walls and red-tiled roof, something Celia found odd but couldn't judge harshly. She rationalized that it could be a pricey blue color only found in Italy, perhaps, because sometimes what you think is tacky is rare and classy in other quarters.

After she parked along the street next to the house, Celia picked a small little gift bag labeled 'Maven Beauty Treats' from the passenger seat. She walked to the front door and gave it three confident knocks.

Nothing.

Celia knocked again, a little louder. Still no response.

She peeped through the glass in the door and, beyond the transparent lace curtain, she saw the form of Mrs. Owens lying on the floor, face up. She wasn't moving. Celia could hear a faint sound seep through - it sounded like music.

Celia's hand started shaking. She was getting anxious wondering if Mrs. Owens was just unconscious or, God forbid the thought, dead.

2

"Hello? Mrs. Owens! Are you okay?" Celia shouted while banging on the front door furiously.

Moments later, and to Celia's surprise, the body started moving. Mrs. Owens' left hand moved to her face slowly. She seemed to be mumbling to herself.

"Mrs. Owens, are you okay?" Celia persisted.

Mrs. Owens tilted her head to the side and asked, "Who's that?"

"It's Celia. I'm here to deliver the beauty products you ordered?"

"Oh, Celia! Give me a moment, let me come over," Mrs. Owens said, getting up gingerly. Celia stepped back from the door to compose herself.

The door lock jingled as it was opened, and Mrs. Owens appeared, wearing a big smile and beaming eyes as if nothing unusual had happened. She had her head wrap tied neatly; her face looked fresh for a woman her age, and she had that graceful aura that announced her presence. Celia was baffled.

"Why didn't I know you were coming this early?" Mrs. Owens asked.

"Well, we had a... anyway, it doesn't matter. Are you okay?" Celia stuttered as she sought to make sense of things.

"Never been better!" Mrs. Owens declared proudly.

"Why were you on the floor?"

"Oh, I'm sorry, there's this new meditation I have been listening to and I drifted off to sleep. Can you believe that?" Mrs. Owens replied with a slight shake of the head.

"Uh, meditation? That's it? Nothing else...?"

"That's it. I am as fit as can be at my age," Mrs. Owens declared.

"Oh. Okay. It must be pretty effective then," Celia said.

"Well, I am not sure about that. It's supposed to clear my mind, not make me sleep. Come on in and make yourself comfortable," Mrs. Owens said as she walked back into the house.

In the living room, Celia noted it was still as cozy and homely as it had always been. Mrs. Owens always had a penchant for memorabilia, and her home was filled with collectibles from years past. Although many were knockoffs, Mrs. Owens gave them the affection one would give to rare masterpieces. There were little sculptures, paintings, postcards, little pendant - bits and pieces that were always conversation starters in Mrs. Owens's home as she often used them to refer to past events in her life. Lately, there were fresh knitted pieces on the couch, which were not memorabilia but simply evidence of Mrs. Owens's newfound hobby: knitting.

Then Celia noticed it: the now pervasive sound of a hypnotic voice, laced with flute music, filling the room.

You are the cat's meow.
Feel the energy of the earth beneath you.
Feel the vibration of the earthworms as they
Massage the soil beneath your skin.
Let nature speak to you...

Celia rolled her eyes as the words of the audio filtered through to her. She found it outrageous, the droning voice of the narrator boring. Adding that snooze fest to the homely feel of the room, Celia understood why Mrs. Owens had drifted off into deep slumber.

"How are the babies?" Mrs. Owens asked, her voice wafting in from the kitchen.

"They are great! Just dropped them off to school," Celia replied.

"They grow so fast, don't they?" Mrs. Owens said as she returned with a mug of hot tea in hand. "Here, sip on this. Is the younger one still quiet?"

"Thanks. He has his moments, but he's doing just fine," Celia replied.

Mrs. Owens then went over to the audio player and switched it off, a merciful gesture to Celia's ears. As she returned, Mrs. Owens got into her trademark story voice, which she often did when relaying a tale.

"You know, I still remember it like yesterday. The day I came to help your mother give birth to you. You were so pretty, just like your mother, and you have passed on that beautiful face and smart mind to your babies. Especially that little boy - little Johnnie. Keep an eye on him. He will have most of the brains, I can guarantee you that."

Celia smiled, she found the thought reassuring. Debt aside, Mrs. Owens held a special place in Celia's heart. She wasn't just a client. She was a close family friend who had been the midwife when Celia was born. As Celia grew up, Mrs. Owens would visit and check on her like a godmother, and Celia had built a healthy affection towards her.

"You have a great mind too and magic hands, Mrs. Owens. Thank you for helping Mama bring me into the world," Celia said.

"Ah stop it, you know I would never have left your mother to her own devices. It was my gift to you," Mrs. Owens gushed, clearly trying to be modest but also loving the fact that her work was recognized. Celia knew that the older she got, the more Mrs. Owens needed such affirmation, and she gave it often. The older woman needed to know that the years gone by still held great significance.

Celia handed the gift bag to Christine Owens, who was smiling with excitement. Mrs. Owens took out her delivery, a matte lipstick and eye shadow that Celia had picked out for her.

"You know the ladies are calling me in for a knitting night. I want to look good," Mrs. Owens beamed.

"You're wearing makeup just for knitting night?" Celia asked quizzically.

"I'll be presenting my latest pieces, so why not? I

have to live it up a little, my girl," Mrs. Owens replied with a little jig. "How much is it?"

"Twenty-five dollars," Celia replied, business-like.

"Twenty-five? For this?" Mrs. Owens seemed genuinely dumbfounded.

"Yes, plus the fifteen dollars you owe from the last delivery. So make it forty dollars."

"You must be joking. How did these become so expensive?" Mrs. Owens asked, still admiring the packaging of the product.

"Umm..."

"I shouldn't be paying so much money to look beautiful. Come on now Celia, give me a better deal."

"That's the best deal I can offer," Celia said, determined not to let the older woman get the best of her.

"I know you can give me a better deal," Mrs. Owens said as she tugged at the heartstrings she knew existed in their relationship.

"Well, I..."

"If that's the case then I better try them on and see.

Keep the tea going," Mrs. Owens said as she disappeared into the bedroom.

Celia sighed and took a sip of the tea. She found it too sweet and wasn't going to ask for a fresh one. She left it and waited. She didn't have to wait long.

Mrs. Owens returned, and she didn't look flattering. She had applied too much lipstick, possibly to make her thinning lips fuller, but they now looked pudgy and crooked. The eye shadow over her eyelids was going in the right direction, but it was not evenly applied, giving her an overall Goth look.

"You always get me the best. I love these! They are so easy to use and my skin is singing songs. Don't you think?" Mrs. Owens asked as she struck a pose in front of Celia.

Celia wondered if the bathroom mirror was broken or the light was dimming because she didn't understand how Mrs. Owens liked her look.

"I…. I agree, the colors suit you perfectly," she said. It wasn't a lie - the shades Celia had chosen were perfect for Mrs. Owens's skin. The application was a different topic, and she wanted to raise her concern respectfully.

"But I think you should tone it down a bit, you know. Keep it simple," Celia found herself saying.

Mrs. Owens turned to her and said, "Simple? Why on earth would I keep it simple? My skin is singing! It's happy! And it says thirty dollars should be enough," Mrs. Owens replied.

Before Celia could protest, Mrs. Owens handed out thirty dollars to her. Celia took it. She thought it would be better to take what she could get and the remaining debt would be recovered somehow. She also needed to evaluate this buyer-seller relationship, because clients like Mrs. Owens would make her go bust, eventually.

"Thank you, Mrs. Owens. I hope you have fun on knitting night."

"Oh, I intend to. The girls will be floored," Mrs. Owens replied.

Celia almost added 'like you were this morning' but she kept it to herself. Instead, she admired how Mrs. Owens spoke, because she spoke those words with the voice and confidence of a movie star.

"Just take your time, don't rush it. And please remember, you can use some foundation." Celia said as she rose to leave.

Celia stopped at the petrol station close by to refuel for the rest of her trips. She had seven more clients to drive to, spread across town. After paying up for the fuel, she walked back to the car. Then she heard a familiar voice behind her.

"Celia?"

Celia turned to see the lively face of Rosie Williams, her former high school mate and great friend, who looked like a model from a holiday magazine.

"Oh wow, Rosie?" Celia said, surprised. Rosie walked over and they embraced.

"If it isn't the ravishing Celia!" Rosie said. She oozed charm, wit and a certain aura of calmness with the world, Celia thought.

"You are visiting?" Celia asked.

"Visiting my hometown? Girl, no! I am saving to do that in the Bahamas if I get there! I moved back home," Rosie replied.

"Seriously? Welcome back!" Celia replied. "Wow, it's been what? Five years since I saw you? You look amazing!"

"Well, you know we have great genes in my family. You look great yourself, my dear," Rosie said.

"Why did you move back?"

"Long story short, my company decided to do a merger. They cut loose the hardest workers like myself and here I am!" Rosie giggled a little. "I want to start something different in a much more relaxed setting. Jo'burg is a bit crazy, I always liked the energy in this place."

"And the holiday spots." Celia chimed.

"Have I ever denied my little pleasures?" Rosie asked. The two women laughed.

"We should catch up sometime," Rosie suggested. "In fact, how about right now?"

Celia shook her head: "Sorry, I can't. I have a few clients waiting to see me."

"What a bummer. Do you know what's cool? I'm throwing a party sometime soon. I'll invite our old friends for a proper catch up! Are you in?" Rosie asked.

"Er, thanks but I am not fun at parties," Celia replied.

What Celia couldn't voice was that she had flashbacks of all the times she had gone out with Rosie in the past. Those times, though a lot of fun, always ended with drama or commotion, and Celia was not keen on having either of those in her life at the moment.

"Well, maybe this is the universe giving you a chance to loosen up. Let off some steam. I think you need it," Rosie winked and smiled. "Trust me, this is not the usual. And I, Rosie Williams, will make it worth your while!"

Celia knew she would give in, eventually. Her gut also knew something out of the ordinary was bound to happen.

3

There is nothing as good as food cooked by your own mother. It doesn't matter which fine dining restaurant you have been to or if the world's best chef took over your kitchen for a day. None of them would be able to put together the bliss that comes from tasting a mother's soul food cooking.

These thoughts were swimming in Celia's mind as she ate her sosatie, the South African kebab. Her taste buds thanked her for each bite she took as she savored every morsel of the grilled lamb meat cubes. Her mother's secret recipe added a subtle lemon flavor to it that reminded Celia of her childhood. This always lifted her spirits.

It had been a long, tiring day, and this was just the kick Celia needed to regain an appreciation of the world. She had met all her clients except one, who suddenly became unavailable at the last minute.

Such surprises happened. She bumped the client onto the next day's list.

Celia had then picked up the boys. They were elated when she stopped by their grandmother's place on the way home. They saw her almost every week, but were always excited as if it were the first time. Celia's mother spoiled the boys like there was no tomorrow.

"Are you really watching your diet or is this an exception?" Audrey Matinise, Celia's buxom, gray-haired mother peered over her glasses as she stared down at her daughter.

"This is sugar-free food, Mama. No sugar is the motto. Everything else is free game," Celia said whilst chewing a small mouthful.

"All right, it's getting out of hand now that you are wolfing them down and talking with your mouth full. You're lucky these boys are not that hungry today," Mrs. Matinise replied with a smile.

Celia smiled back. She looked through the large living room windows facing the rear lawn, where she could see the boys playing an improvised form of football with a leather ball that their grandmother had just given to them as a gift.

"They haven't discovered the magic your food has.

I'm taking it in because I know from experience what it can do," Celia said with a glint in her eye.

"I know what it can do. We never age here. Our good genes don't run out," Mrs. Matinise said.
"Watch my skin glow after this! This food is the secret people are missing out on in this world," Celia said.

Mrs. Matinise burst out laughing. Celia loved the way she could banter with her mother about anything. If it wasn't for the age difference, you could easily think the two were sisters. They would talk about anything under the sun; nothing was off limits. Celia was relaxed here. Perhaps it was the years of experience working as a nurse where she skillfully comforted patients that made Mrs. Matinise so good at putting someone at ease. It was at those moments, when your guard was down, that she would ask sensitive questions.

"So, has my beautiful daughter been on a date recently?" Mrs. Matinise asked.

Celia hated these questions, but she knew she couldn't avoid them.
"Mama, we saw each other last week and I told you no," she said.

"A lot can change in a week. Heck, a lot can happen in a day!" Mrs. Matinise replied with a chuckle.

"Nothing has changed here. I'm too busy with the boys and the business," Celia said, keeping her tone as matter-of-fact as possible. Mrs. Matinise moved closer to her.

"It's been five years, Celia. He would have wanted you to move on."

"I'm doing that, Mama. I'm building the life that we envisioned together," Celia said, agitated.

Silence. It was clear that they both had a fondness for Trevor. His presence had been larger than life, and it wasn't just because of his size. His large voice filled rooms with mirth and energy because he loved telling stories and making fun of the people around him. For a big man with the tactical nous to battle an army, he had been a gentle bear to his loved ones. When Celia had gotten the call that there had been 'an incident'- that's what they called it - she had dashed to the army headquarters. In her mind, Celia figured he might have been injured in combat, something that they had always talked about. As she drove, she had replayed the changes she would make to the house as he recovered: taking out the wheelchair from the basement if he couldn't walk, or use the crutches if it wasn't too serious. The gazebo they had built at the back that overlooked the forest would have needed some cleaning, nothing serious. He would use it when he went to get some fresh air. The first aid kit was there, the medicine cabinet was stocked with painkillers just in case, but maybe his doctor might recommend another type of drug. She had upgraded the medical insurance coverage and knew they would be safe with the expenses. Growing up, Celia had learned the many ways of nursing a patient at home by literally helping her mother out whenever one of the other family members was bedridden at home. She was ready for this moment.

Until she realized she actually was not ready. Trevor had been killed in combat. She would never hear his voice again.

She was shattered for the next couple of weeks after she got the news. Even after his funeral, which was led by the military in honor of him, she had struggled to cope. Her mother always feared Celia barely had time to mourn Trevor's death, and the fact that she had never dated again was a very clear indicator to her that Celia had not moved on. She may have retired as a nurse, but she was still in the nursing business. She was determined to ease Celia over the line.

"I'm not asking you to rush into anything," Mrs. Matinise said.
"Why didn't you remarry?" Celia countered. Her father had died of cancer fifteen years ago, and her mother had never walked down the aisle again.

"Well, have you forgotten Mr. Awesome?" Mrs.

Matinise asked. Celia hadn't. He had been Mrs. Matinise's partner for years after her father's death, but lately she had not seen much of him.

"I haven't actually – where is he?"

"He's out there on a cruise ship somewhere, chasing his bucket list," Mrs. Matinise said. "I won't be waiting for him, but I still have a thing for that silly man," she said fondly.

"How do you cope?"

"Take it one day at a time. Then remember there is nothing wrong to feel that you miss a man in your life. Trevor filled a man-shaped hole in your life. Another man can do the same," she said.

"I'm not sure there's a man who can fill that shape like he did," Celia confessed.

"Maybe. But you will never know until you go on those dates," Mrs. Matinise advised. Celia could see the sense in the point being made. She just didn't have the energy to start looking.

"How's the business going," Mrs. Matinise asked, changing the subject.

"Busy. I had a very active day with deliveries, only missed one. Tomorrow we go again."

"Good, good. Take every chance you get to grow it. Save, invest. Multiply."

"Trust me, that's the goal. Going to have an empire in a few years," Celia said.

Mrs. Matinise smiled and said, "You remind me so much of my younger self. You go out and get things done. You're better at it than I was - you focus and don't let go until it comes to pass. I'm proud of you."

"Thank you. That means a lot to me," Celia said with a wide smile. She didn't mind some positive affirmation.

"On that note, I think you deserve some more sosatie," Mrs. Matinise said as she turned to the kitchen.

"Wait, there's more? Why didn't you tell me?" Celia exclaimed.

"With your rate of eating, do you think it would have been wise to share my backup plan with you?" Mrs. Matinise asked with a wry smile.

Celia laughed. Then her phone rang. It was Rosie. Mrs. Matinise disappeared into the kitchen.

"Heya, Celia! How are you doing, girl?" Rosie asked.

"I'm great thanks. Long day," Celia said.

"Don't worry, I have just the thing to make you relax a little more! So, I've come up with a date for the party. We'll have it this Saturday, from three o'clock till late. Or maybe till the night is done, who knows? You should come though," Rosie said with confidence.

"Sorry Rosie, you remember parties are not my thing…"

"Relax! It's going to be a really small group, you know. People with a good head on their shoulders. A really sober group. Actually, they might not be sober at the end of the night," Rosie chuckled, "but you know what I mean."
"Rosie, I really can't," Celia said.

Rosie interrupted her. "Okay, hear me out. How about I make it a party where the theme is makeup? You can sell your products to the guests who will come. You get to party while making money. What could be more perfect?"

Rosie had a point. A makeup-themed party would work to Celia's advantage. It was worth a shot, if the crowd was in the money. With Rosie, it most likely was.

"Hmm. Tell me who's coming," Celia said.

"I'm still building the final list but I am sure you will

love it."

"I just want to know who will be coming. Come on now," Celia persisted.

"Where's the fun in that? I'll be there in case you have no one to talk to," Rosie said.

"Please…"
"Come on over, Celia. It will be a surprise you have been longing for," Rosie said, knowing she already had Celia on the hook. The game was sealed.

Celia hated surprises, and this was not going to change. Yet, she was going to go for it. After all, she had survived the morning scare with Mrs. Owens. What's the worst that could happen?

4

Celia drove up to the large mansion off Manor Street. The William's family home was still as imposing as she could remember it. The gate opened on its own as she got close, activated by motion sensors, and Celia could feel the aura of wealth seep into the car. The sound of her wheels rolling gently over the gravel added to the ambience of the whistling trees on either side of the long driveway.

At the car park were a few high-end cars: a Maserati, a Porsche and a BMW sports car. Her family station wagon was immaculately maintained and had decent power under its hood, but it was at a lower price point comparatively. She still parked next to them because she was not fazed by such opulence. Celia was walking up to the large main door, pulling her suitcase with products behind her, when Rosie came running towards her.

"Aaand she's here!" Rosie shouted as she hugged Celia. "It's really good to see you."

"Thanks for having me," Celia replied with a smile. "Where do I set up?"

"That's why you're early, huh? Always the prepared one. Come with me."

Rosie led Celia through the large hallway that led to the party room. Celia had fond memories of her teens when she used to visit Rosie's home. She never understood how people lived in a house big enough to have its own party room.

"I remember coming here to watch movies and your father used to get us that huge tub of strawberry ice cream to dig into," Celia said.
"Oh yeah! Those were fun times! You want to check out the movie room again?" Rosie asked.

"Ah no, not now. I just like good memories."

"I hear you girl, I hear you!" Rosie said.

The party room was huge. It had a high ceiling, large windows overlooking the lush gardens outside, round tables and seats for guests, a serving area, a small dance floor, and a DJ booth. It was soundproofed from wall to wall by carpets and rugs from the William's family business; they were leading manufacturers of everything carpets and rugs, and you could tell from the quality that they knew their job well. Along one end of the wall where a series of tables with little colorful umbrellas atop them.

Rosie, pointing at the tables, said: "So we set up these spots for you and anyone else who wants to put up their products during the party."

"You said it's a small party. Why are we in such a big room?" Celia asked.

"It is a small party. Only twenty people are coming."

"So why are we in such a big room? We could easily..."

"Ssssh, watch," Rosie said. She moved to the wall that had a series of switches. She flipped two of them at once and there was a subtle whirring sound that came from the middle of the room.

Suddenly, Celia noticed the large partition panels that stood on each side of the room. The panels moved towards each other at a slow but steady pace. A minute later, the panels had joined to form a temporary wall. They were now standing in a much smaller room whose table seating was just shy of thirty people.

"There you go. Looks more like it, huh?" Rosie asked.

"I am impressed," Celia responded.

"Great! Feel at home. Need some help to set up?"

"No, it's nothing complicated, I'll be fine," Celia replied, setting the case next to her stand.

"Are you sure about that?' a familiar male voice asked from behind them, and the two women turned to see the new arrival. Standing there was the tall form of Mark Williams, Rosie's older brother. He was dressed smartly in a sweater, cotton shirt and jeans. Celia could tell he was in great shape. He smiled, activating his dimples.

"Hey Mark! Guess who's here, a blast from the past!" Rosie said animatedly.

"You mean a bombshell from the past," Mark said with a glint in his eyes. "Hello Celia. Good to see you."

"Hello Mark," Celia replied, her smile trying to mask a slight blush. "You look well."

"I am well, thank you. Yourself?"

"I'm great, thanks. Here for the party."

"Yes, Rosie told me about it."

Noticing the tension of past bonds weighing in, Rosie took her cue to leave.

"While the two of you catch up, let me meet up with the other guests. Someone should be bringing you some wine in a few, to get you into the mood. See ya!" With that, Rosie strutted off.

Celia wanted to stop Rosie from leaving, but it was too late. Why? Well, she shared with Mark an unspoken feeling of unfinished business since their high school romance, which ended abruptly.

"Rosie tells me the beauty consultancy business is thriving these days," Mark said.

"Yes, yes. It's pretty established now. It feels easier making other people look and feel beautiful." Celia said.

"That's a great thing, giving other people a better version of themselves."

"Well, it's not superhero level work, but it does make a difference in its own way I think," Celia remarked, keen to manage expectations. "What are you up to these days?"
"I run the family business now. My parents are getting older, and they asked me to leave my practice and step in. So that's the latest news," Mark replied. As he spoke, Celia noticed that his hand didn't bear a wedding ring.

"Do you like it?" Celia asked.

"Yes, I have grown to enjoy it. It's like a mission," he said. Hearing Mark say this made Celia's endorphins spike. She liked a man with a purpose.

"I'll get you that wine while you set up, okay?" Mark offered.

"Sounds good," Celia replied. As he walked away, she imagined what it would be like if she was walking next to him, hand in hand, as his wife. What would it have been like, becoming a member of this family, if they had eloped as they said they would?

At exactly three o'clock, all the guests had arrived. Apart from the occasional figure of Mark and some servers, the space was full of ladies. They were all former school mates from Happy Springs High, although there were quite a number that Celia didn't know. She could recognize Sheila, whose father ran the local pharmacy where they would go to buy lollipops. Samantha Bradley, who was Miss Happy Springs two years in a row and was still sporting her slender, model-like form after all these years. Celia had bumped into her a few times in town, though they never talked much. Karen Damonze, the local church minister's daughter who was a talented singer. She was now married to the successful banker Dennis Damonze and living the good life. The last person she recognized was Azzara Basson, who had competed for the Miss Happy Springs crown once, but lost to Samantha. She was now running her own successful catering business that catered to high-end clients like the Williams' family. She too had a stand two tables away from Celia's, with an assortment of delectable finger food for guests.

There was throwback music playing from their high school days. The guests filled the room with chatter while they talked in small groups as servers moved around pouring drinks and offering food bites. The atmosphere was alive and kicking, and Celia was ready for it. She had decided instead of offering just free samples, she would give quick makeup sessions to any lady interested in her products. If they believed in the product after seeing how good it looked on them, they would buy it. She was here to close the deal, not just show off her range.
Celia joined a group of five women chatting close to her and listened in.

"It was out of this world! A whole giraffe poked its head into the restaurant and wanted to have my breakfast," Samantha said animatedly. She traveled a lot and always had tales of her adventures at her fingertips for such social settings.
 "You're lying to us, come on! A giraffe's head through a window?" Karen asked. Celia noted how Karen's hairdo was simple but elegant. Her jewelry and mannerism were that of a lady who was definitely married, but not tied down by it.

"Now why would I lie to you, Karen? Wait, I have

some pictures," Samantha said as she lifted the phone she was holding and scrolled through it for a few seconds. "There you go. See! And I don't have Photoshop on here, if you care to dig in further!"

Samantha passed her phone around as each of the women took a quick glance at the photograph. There was a mishmash of reactions that included:

'unbelievable!'
'oh, he's so big and cute.'
'look at those eyes.'
'this is so romantic.'
'why is it so close to the food?'
'did you eat afterwards?'

Karen, who had stirred up this quest for evidence, didn't look amused by Samantha's evidence and resulting vindication.

"Excuse me ladies, I have to go freshen up a little," Karen said and left.

When the phone got to Celia, she was taken in by the frame: Samantha was posed with the giraffe quite close to her. She was alone, although there were two plates at the table. It was most likely that her partner had taken the photograph for her - it was none of Celia's business to know who this was because the whole town knew Samantha had never been close to marrying. Celia envied this life; it

looked like the kind of place Trevor would have taken her for a getaway, as they both loved traveling and trying out new restaurants. It was one of the things she missed about him not being around anymore.
"Where was this?" Celia asked.

"It's a cute restaurant in Nairobi, Kenya. We had gone on safari there. What an experience!" Samantha gushed. Celia handed back the phone.

"I am famished! Where are those food trays?" Samantha asked.

"But I thought you just ate a whole chicken, going by the number of drumsticks you have eaten?" Celia joked.

"Did you see how tiny those drumsticks were? They can hardly be considered an appetizer! Besides, I have been on this intermittent fasting plan for the last seven days and my, oh my, the cravings I get sometimes!" Samantha said.

"You eat so much, yet we don't see where the food goes!" another lady named Melanie said. They laughed.

"It's always been the same story since high school, Melanie, it's not going to change!" Samantha chuckled. "Let me head to Azzara's table and get some bites. I'll be back."

Samantha stepped out of the group and headed towards Azzara's stand. Celia was trying to recall Melanie's face from her memory of high school girls, but she couldn't remember her. Melanie seemed quiet and organized, and possibly one of those who talked more once she had a little wine. Celia made a note to get to know her as the evening wore on. Meanwhile, Celia decided to fill up the silence with a quick pitch.

"Hey ladies, I'm selling some high-quality beauty products and wanted to give you a free makeup session. Doesn't hurt to try, so who wants in?" Celia said.
"I'm game!" Melanie was the first to say. Two more ladies raised their hands.

"All right! Come on over before the word gets out!" Celia said. Eager volunteers were a good sign.

Celia led the women to her stand. She started working on Melanie, who had thinned out her eyebrows and hardly wore lipstick. Celia decided it would be great to fill out her eyebrows slightly and apply some gloss that suited her thin lips. As she did this, she learned that her full name was Melanie Dawes. She worked as a librarian at the town library, which had been recently modernized. Five minutes later, Melanie looked at her reflection and was ecstatic.

"Oh, my word. Celia, you are a genius. How did you do that?" she asked.

"I have a knack for knowing which colors and blends would work on any complexion," Celia replied.

"You're an artist! I have to buy this," Melanie said as she struck different poses in front of a large mirror as if she had never seen herself before. Celia knew she had her in the bag.
Just then, Samantha appeared. She was stuffing two fish fingers into her mouth with gusto.

"How about me, Celia?" Samantha asked.

"Come on Samantha, we both know you don't like makeup," Celia replied.

"That's true, but it doesn't mean I don't use it. Sometimes when doing a fashion show, you just have to. Anyway, I just had a few bites, and I need a retouch. Just a little. Some powder here and there. Maybe some gloss too, just like Melanie's?"

Melanie smiled awkwardly and shrugged, "I don't mind sharing a good look."

Celia looked at the other ladies who were waiting, and they waved her on, signaling their readiness to wait.

Celia waved to Samantha and said, "Have a seat, my dear."

"Awesome!" she said, moving fast into the seat. For someone who couldn't stand makeup, Celia admired her enthusiasm.

Noticing Melanie staring at some of the products on her stand, she said, "I think you should definitely get some gloss and eyeliners plus some foundation. It really looks good on you."

"Do you have a free sample of the foundation I could try out first?" Melanie asked.

"Oh, yes. After I am done with Samantha and the two ladies, I will prep your order," she replied.

"Thanks a bunch!" Melanie said as she left to join the party. Minutes later, Celia finished the transformation work she had begun on Samantha.

"You're really good at this, Celia. I'm usually careful about what I put on my face because my skin is sensitive, but this right here is a winner!" she said.

"You're welcome. You want to buy some?"

"Buy some? Do you have packs of this stuff? Because I would like to buy in bulk and forget about it!" Samantha said confidently. Celia couldn't be happier.

"Sure, why not! I may have to get some more stock in and have it delivered to your house," she said.

"Yes, that sounds like fun. And we can catch up, I can have you over for lunch," Samantha said. Celia briefly marveled at the prospect she may be reconnecting with someone she had never really known well. They exchanged numbers for the first time, and Celia promised to call once the order was ready for delivery.

"Let's take a quick picture before the day gets wild," Samantha said. They posed for a selfie together. They must have taken eight different poses before Samantha was satisfied. "Got it!"

Samantha sauntered away into the party crowd as Celia worked on the other ladies.
Fifteen minutes later Celia was done and decided to take a short break. She walked to the now larger group of women as they flaunted their spruced-up looks. Her work had created a buzz and five other women raised their hands. Celia was excited that her effort was paying off.

"Ladies, don't do dinner before I pamper you a little. We all know that it will be hard to do that after the food and wine takes a hold!" Celia teased, and they laughed.

"We should all take pictures after this," one of them

said.

"Yes, we should. Samantha is our resident photographer. Where is she?" Celia asked.

No one could spot Samantha after looking around the room, and Celia hoped she had not rushed to the bathroom to remove the makeup - she had been careful to apply it sparingly.
Moments later, Rachel Bass, who was the daughter of one of the town's former councilors, rushed into the room, out of breath.

"Hey, which of you here is a doctor or knows advanced first aid?" she asked.
"I know first aid," Celia replied. "Why, what's going on?"

"Just come with me," Rachel said as she turned around. Celia followed her quickly.

"What's going on?" Celia prodded.

"I think Samantha has been drinking or something. She's fainted on the stairs," Rachel replied hurriedly.

When they got to the stairs, they found Mark administering CPR to the still form of Samantha.

"Have you called an ambulance?" Mark bellowed.

"Calling one now!" Rachel replied as she pressed her phone frantically.

"Stop slacking, this is serious!" Mark shouted.

Celia got to Mark. "Can I help you out?" she asked.

"No, hold back for now. Look out for that ambulance!" he replied. He was tense, constantly monitoring Samantha's face for any response. "Come on, Sam! Come on!"

Five minutes later, with Mark a little winded, Celia took over. She had learned emergency life-saving skills at the age of nine, as her mother had been keen for everyone in their household to know what it took to save someone's life.

Celia was ready for this moment. However, it was very obvious to her from the moment she touched her body that Samantha Bradley was already dead.

5

There were only twenty guests at the party, but this unexpected scenario made her more acutely aware that most of them had been sheltered from the hazards of life. They were detached from things like sudden deaths and emergencies, so most of them didn't know what to do except succumb to overreaction and anxiety.

Some women were crying, their makeup washing out under a stream of tears; others were frozen speechless; others were moving around trying to be active due to the adrenaline pumping in their veins, but were not aiding the situation.

Celia had continued administering CPR to Samantha's body for a few more minutes as she waited for the paramedics to arrive. When they got there, they did their best to revive her. They checked Samantha's pulse and vitals, attached an oxygen mask to her face before rushing her out on a stretcher to the ambulance that had drenched the car park with flashing lights. The paramedics had a brief chat with Mark before speeding off towards the hospital. Mark then broke the news to everyone that Samantha was gone, asking everyone not to text anyone or post anything on social media before he could notify her next of kin, which Celia found quite considerate.

As the gravity of the events dawned on everyone, speculation began about what happened. Had she been unwell? Had she been pushed down the stairs by someone? Was it the food she ate at Azzara's food table? Celia listened to the whispers and shook her head. The human mind always looks to make meaning out of what it does not understand, while it's always better to lean on facts. But facts can take time to reveal themselves, and human beings are not always patient.

At this point, another siren drew closer to the house, and there was reduced chatter as they realized it was the police. A policeman in plain clothes and wearing a heavy coat secured the scene. He started interviewing each person, writing their statements in his thick brown notebook. He was later joined by an entourage of officers. The place swarmed with them as the evening set in.

Once Celia had given her statement, she asked if she could leave because she needed to get to her boys. The policeman agreed, but refused to let her take down the setup of her beauty products display. Other stands, including Azzara's, were almost down before they were stopped.

"Am I a suspect?" Celia asked.

"At this point, everyone here is a suspect. This whole house and everything in it is a crime scene, so you cannot take anything out in case it is evidence," the policeman answered.

"That doesn't make sense. Then why are you letting me leave?" Celia asked.

"Well, I have already checked you. At least when I need to find you, I can find you. Your stick of lipstick doesn't have an address. On that note, please come to the station at nine o'clock tomorrow morning. Thanks," the policeman quipped and went away.

Celia walked past the huddled guests and the many police officers who were taking pictures of the scene and collecting samples. She was glad to be able to get away from it all. As she left, she saw Rosie and Mark watching the proceedings with serious expressions. She decided not to weigh them down with questions; she would check on them the next morning.

Later that night, after tucking in her sons, Celia couldn't help wondering which party guest wanted

Samantha dead - and why did they choose the party as the best place to do it?

6

The next morning was a Sunday, and Celia usually used it as a day to recharge and connect with the boys. However, she wouldn't be able to do that with them for the rest of the day. She was going to be at the police station, and judging from stories she had heard, it was possible she would spend the entire day there, giving statements and answering more questions.

Celia drove her sons to her mother's house and found Mrs. Matinise waiting outside. She looked radiant in a colorful sundress that Celia had helped pick out when they went for one of their monthly mother-daughter shopping sprees. They would just randomly wake up on those days and decide if they were going to shop for clothes or groceries or the best deals in town. It was something they both enjoyed doing and gave them an opportunity to spend time together.

"Where are my boys?" Mrs. Matinise asked as the car came to a stop. The boys rushed out and gave her a hug as she laughed. "You better not push me over now."

Celia walked up to her mother and added her embrace to the mix.

"So are you finally going on that date we talked about?" Mrs. Matinise teased. For the first time, Celia wished she could say 'yes, I am!' because a date was definitely a more exciting prospect than spending a day with the local police.

Instead, she shook her head and said, "I have an appointment."

"With a client? On a Sunday morning?" Mrs. Matinise asked. Celia shook her head again. The two women locked eyes and her mother knew something was up.

"Boys, get into the house and set up the table. Grandma's got a surprise for you," she said.

"All right! Bye Mom!" the boys said as they dashed into the house.

"Bye boys, and don't eat too much of Grandma's goodies!" Celia replied.

As soon as they were out of earshot, Mrs. Matinise

said, "Well?"

"I have to go to the police station. I'm simply making a statement."
"What's going on, Cece?" Mrs. Matinise asked, her eyes furrowed in concern.

"I'm okay, I just have to give a statement," Celia was trying to make light of it, but her mother was having none of it.

"Answer the question."

Celia sighed. "Someone died at the party yesterday. They're interviewing everyone who attended."

"Someone died and you're acting as if nothing happened? Is this when you tell me?" Mrs. Matinise asked angrily.

"It's nothing mom. I have to go. Let's talk about it later?" Celia pleaded.

"All right. Take care of yourself, and if you need me to come and get you, just call. Okay?" she said.
Celia nodded with a weak smile. She got into her car and drove off.

Bill Koloane was not what Celia expected her interrogator to look like. He was clean-shaven, but with a goatee that was trimmed down to precision.

His bald head shone in the overhead light, and she could guess that he shaved it two to three times a week. His shirt, though having rolled-up sleeves, was well-pressed and his trousers were fitting. His shoes were so shiny you could see your reflection on them. He was clearly a man who looked after himself, perhaps a little too much for a policeman. She admired it, but on his salary, she was suspicious of his ethics.

She was tired of him. Detective Koloane had been asking her detailed questions for the past forty-five minutes and there was no letup. Celia had told him everything she knew, breaking down how events unfolded from the time she had arrived at the Williams' house to the moment the first policeman arrived and questioned her. Every bit, right up to the time she watched her sons turn in for the night.

"All right, you don't have to tell me more. I was only trying to understand the sequence of events and all witnesses are giving their accounts so we can crosscheck the information," Detective Koloane said.

"So, you will come and interview my sons to prove I was home? They are not part of this," she said.

"No, we won't need to do that," he reassured her.

Atop the table where they sat in the small, sparse, gray-walled room was a small portable audio recorder. During pauses where Detective Koloane would write his notes, she could hear it whirring.

"Why would there be a makeup themed party?" Detective Koloane asked. He looked genuinely baffled.

"It was Rosie's idea. She knows how hard I work on the business. We hadn't connected for a while, and she thought it would be a great way to give my operation a boost. Introducing the product to a new line of clients is something I always try to do. This was a great way to do it," Celia explained.

"Judging from what you said earlier, you wanted to make sales at the party?" he asked.

"Yes, sharing my brand with new customers and closing sales is what I do. It's just that the setting varies sometimes."

"And you were one of the last people to interact with Samantha. Tell me this, why did you apply makeup on her, yet it's generally known that she doesn't like makeup?" he asked, his tone cutting like a knife through the air.
Celia didn't hesitate, "I was aware of it, and I asked her the same question. But she wanted to do it. Even as I met her request, we agreed to only apply it sparingly. I kept any potentially harmful ingredients away from her."

"Are you sure you succeeded?" he asked.

"Yes. I mean, I literally asked her what suited her and what didn't and she told me," Celia replied.

Silence. Detective Koloane scribbled some more notes. As the recorder whirred, she grew nervous. Why was he asking her trick questions? What was he getting at?

"Am I a suspect here?" Celia asked.

Detective Koloane looked up at her as if irritated with the boldness of her question.

"Everyone is a suspect. I think you were told that yesterday. No one has been cleared, not until we get the toxicology report from the lab," Detective Koloane said.

"Am I under arrest?"

"For now, no. Will you be arrested at some point within the next forty-eight, or ninety-six hours? Maybe," he said, matter-of fact.

"I see," she replied. Celia didn't like where the conversation was going.

"We will most likely call you in again tomorrow," Detective Koloane added.

As that played in her mind, she hoped she wouldn't need to call her mother to come get her. Then she realized that if she was arrested on suspicion of murder, she would have to call her mother to go get the boys, because she wouldn't be returning home.

7

"Nothing like a little fresh air and sun to shake off that morning," Celia said to herself as she walked down the main street.

She had survived the interrogation, but was not amused by how Detective Koloane had handled the interview. It's times like these that you look at your own record with law enforcement, just to prove to yourself what kind of citizen you have been. She had never fallen foul of the police, usually working with the philosophy that cooperating with them was better than trying to be a hero. She had never had to defend her innocence, except maybe the time when she rear-ended another driver at a stoplight, which was actually caused by her starting her car while her foot wasn't on the brake pedal. Rookie mistake.

Detective Koloane had hounded her somewhat, and she wondered if this was the same thing he was doing to each witness, just to see who would break. Maybe it was strategic in that way, but she'd also been informed that the police had no strong leads on who actually did it. They were shaking every branch as hard as they could until a fruit dropped.

As Celia walked past the large window of a coffee shop, she looked inside and saw a familiar figure. She slowed down as she tried to confirm if what she was seeing was true.

Seated in one of the better tables was Rosie, and she was talking animatedly on her phone like someone who was narrating a very exciting story. She then laughed with great mirth, and this struck Celia. Why was the host whose party was ruined by a possible murder this happy just a few hours after the incident?

Celia had to talk to Rosie, so she walked into the coffee shop. She went to the self-service counter first and ordered an Americano coffee. Once served, she walked straight to where Rosie sat. Rosie was still having her animated phone call.

"...you had better come through, my dear," Rosie said as she noticed Celia arrive. "I've got to go now. Let's talk soon and toast to this new adventure, okay? Thanks. Ciao!"

"Hey Rosie," Celia said. "Didn't think I would find you here."

"Celia! Small world they say, huh? Come on, have a seat!" Rosie said with a smile. She was having a masala tea and chocolate doughnuts, one of which was already half eaten.

"Are you okay?" Celia asked.

"Yeah, sure! I mean, a little tired after yesterday. We slept quite late because the police stayed on for hours after it happened. Told you that it would be a surprise," Rosie said.

Celia wasn't sure if Rosie was excited that it happened, or just confirming that she had a thing for attracting trouble.

"That you did, that you did. You look, er, happy and refreshed though," Celia said.

"Well, life is short. It's a new day, and my conscience is clear about the whole thing," Rosie said nonchalantly.

"How can your conscience be clear? Someone died in your house," Celia said, trying to wrap her head around it.

"Yeah, but life happens. I didn't do it, and that's the truth. They will find the person who did it, I'm sure."

"Yeah, but a life was lost. Someone you know. That's

what I meant. You feel nothing about that?" Celia prodded.

"I do feel bad that it happened at my place, sure. But does that change anything? It's a pity I didn't know Samantha very well, other than the fact she worked at an animal shelter. Paws and Whiskers, I think it's called. I liked that about her, because I'm an animal lover myself. Also, everyone knows I don't handle death very well, so there's that too," Rosie said as she bit into her doughnut.

If Rosie had done it, then she had the perfect mindset of a murderer, Celia thought. But she couldn't bring herself to believe that it would be Rosie. She wouldn't have done it at a party she organized herself - that would be counterproductive to the idea of getting away with it.

"Did the cops mess up my stuff?" Celia asked.

"Oh, yeah. Don't worry, nothing was seized, except a stick of lip gloss, I think. I had one of my people pack them for you. They can be dropped off later today at your place. Just send me your address," Rosie offered.

"That would be great, thanks. Also, there were some guests at the party I couldn't remember and we apparently went to school together. Karen, I can remember. Melanie, I had no idea about her at all.

Do you mind filling me in some more?" Celia asked.

"Well, Karen Summers was a bookworm in school, always in the library and scoring high grades. She's now married to the Spiro bank manager. Very stylish couple," Rosie said.

"Yeah, I know a bit about that. I could tell from her outfit and accessories that they seem to have a bit of money," she replied.

"Not a bit, a lot. Well, not as much as my family, of course, but quite a lot. They've been married for a few years and are making good moves around the place. Power couple with the perfect life," Rosie said.

For someone who knew how those circles worked, Rosie's description fit perfectly with what Celia suspected.

"Karen didn't seem too impressed with Samantha at times," Celia said.

"Karen is like that. I guess it's an introvert thing. She never mingles comfortably, so one time she's all warm and friendly, then she suddenly pulls away. I wouldn't read much into it. She does it to everybody," Rosie said. Celia agreed - not everyone can handle social situations in the same way.

Rosie continued, "Melanie Dawes works at the local

library. She's a great librarian, been there a few times to check it out. Great spot to slow down the day with a book."

"Is she married?" Celia asked.

"No, she's single. Maybe the library scene doesn't have good suitors," Rosie said.

Or it's a personal choice, Celia wanted to say.

"How about Azzara? The one who runs the catering business," Celia enquired.

"Azzara is amazing. She didn't come from a rich family, but her father ran a restaurant. It's still there, I think. I guess that's where she got the idea for the catering business. She works with some of the top establishments and names here. Parties, events, you name it. She can get you the food you need to make it special. Miracle worker," she enthused.

"Those are glowing accolades. Tell me something, do you think she did it?"

"Azzara? Why would she? Other than the fact they were not really good friends in high school after the whole Miss Happy Springs thing, I don't see why. That's really not a reason to kill someone years later, right?" Rosie posed.

Celia shrugged. She agreed. It didn't make sense that a high school grudge over a fashion competition would trigger a murder years later.

"But, hey! I never thought that someone could be murdered at my house and voila! So, life is full of surprises," Rosie added with a laugh. Celia couldn't help smiling too, because the world did seem to have a twisted sense of humor.

"Yeah, not everyone is a methodical killer. I just hope that there are some clues out there," Celia said.

"Are you an investigator now? That's how much you loved it at the police station?" Rosie teased. Celia laughed.

"Don't remind me about that. Look, I have to go. Let me recover what little is left of my day. Good to see you," Celia said as she got up.

"Should I pass any message to Mark?" Rosie asked with a sly wink.

"No, not today. I'll see him when I see him," she replied.

As Celia left Rosie to her masala and chocolate doughnut feast, her mind was still unsettled. Maybe it was the pressure she was getting from the police, or her own conscience that wanted to solve this. She was determined to find answers from somewhere.

8

The next morning was slightly overcast, making it a cooler morning than usual. Though she was not superstitious, Celia hoped it was not the proverbial gathering of clouds before a storm.

As promised, Rosie had sent her driver to drop off Celia's products the evening before. Everything was intact except the ones she had used for the sessions and the single stick of lip gloss taken by the police for lab testing.

It was already mid-morning and Celia hadn't received a call from Detective Koloane. She took that as a good sign. The boys were at school, and she had already gotten an order from a long-standing client to deliver some makeup to her salon. The day was picking up nicely, and she intended to go about it as normal.

Celia went through her inventory, arranging the products her client needed for delivery. She needed to restock soon. Fortunately, the head office had confirmed that her order had been processed and she would replenish supplies the following week. She then remembered Samantha had wanted to make a big order too, and that made her heart sink a little.

Her delivery package set and ready, Celia freshened up. It was as she was checking herself for the last time in the mirror while humming a tune that she heard footsteps coming up to her door. She paused, not sure if she was hearing it right. Just then, a leaflet was pushed underneath her door. The footsteps went away.

She walked to the door and looked through the peephole to see who it was. She saw no one.

She picked up the leaflet. It read:

'Paws and Whiskers Animal Shelter invites you to an Open Week! Pop in any day of the week and get the chance to connect with the sweetest animals in town!'

She remembered that it was the same animal shelter Rosie had talked about at the coffee shop. While Celia wasn't a big believer in serendipity, she took this as a sign that she needed to go there. She grabbed her car keys along with the delivery package and left.

Driving back from the successful delivery, Celia drove up along Bay Street. It was not the busiest street, and most establishments were wholesalers. It would be easier to get a space here for an animal shelter, she figured, as the land rates would be cheaper than other parts of town. She hadn't driven for very long when she saw the large sign: Paws and Whiskers Animal Shelter. She turned into it. The front of the shelter had a decent parking area, with two Land cruiser pickups parked at the front, bearing the shelter's logo. She guessed the animals would be at the back. The shop colors were bright and designed to give you that warm, welcoming feeling.

The door jingled as she walked in. At the counter was a young receptionist, probably in her early twenties. She had a green polo shirt with the shelter's logo, and her hair was tied in a cute bun.

"Hello, welcome to Paws and Whiskers! I'm Brenda. Which of our little friends are you interested in seeing today?" the receptionist asked, wearing the widest smile. She looked genuinely happy to see a visitor.

"Er, it's my first time here so I'm open to whatever you propose," Celia said.

"Do you have a pet? Any animals you like in particular?" Brenda asked.

"I like most animals. Except bugs, bats, snakes, slugs and any wildlife that needs to be in the wild," Celia said with a chuckle.

Brenda laughed back. She took out a printed list of animals that lay next to a thick, blue folder. Next to each name was a small image of the animal.

"So this is a list of the animals we have at the moment. Most of them have been saved from cruel owners, or from the streets. Many of them were not in the best condition when we found them, but we have nurtured them well."

"The ones you have on this list are the ones you have looked after, treated and are now ready to have a new home?"

"Yeah, we can't give out the ones that just came in until we have treated them and at least helped them recover from whatever difficulty they were facing," she replied.

It sounded like a great place for an animal to get a second chance at life. Celia wondered if this good-natured girl even knew what had happened to Samantha.

"So, which of these darlings stand out to you? Which one can you recommend?" Celia asked.

"Wow, that's a tough one. I'm a little new in this part of the business. Another colleague of mine would have been perfect for this, but she's not around at the moment," Brenda replied.

"This other colleague, would her name be Samantha by any chance?"

"Yeah, Sammy. You know her?"

"Yes, we actually went to high school together back in the day," she said.

"She was great with all the animals. Sammy would tell you anything you needed to know."

"Can you tell me more about Samantha? What was she like, what work she did, that kind of stuff?" Celia asked.

"Um, well. I'm not sure I should..." Brenda started to say.

"Who's that asking about Samantha?" a deep voiced bellowed from the back.

Celia angled her neck over Brenda's shoulder as she looked for the source of the voice. She saw a hairy, bespectacled man's head pop out from behind a stack of wooden crates.

"I was just asking her..." Celia started to say, but he cut her off.

"Wrong answer. I asked you this: who wants to know?"

9

"My name is Celia Dube, and you must be the manager," Celia replied.

"Come on over to my office, Ms. Dube, and let's talk," the man said to her. Brenda pointed to a little space through which Celia walked past the counter and to the back. Hidden by the stacked crates was a door leading to a spacious, neat office. It had a wide office table full of paperwork. The walls had posters of animals and pin-ups of activity sheets. Two chairs stood next to the table.

The man, who was stocky and hairy on his arms, ushered her towards a seat. Celia eased into it while he sat across from her, training his suspicious gaze on her.

"So, what brings you fishing here about Samantha?" the man asked.

"Samantha was a friend of mine. We went to high

school together. Who, may I ask, am I speaking to?" Celia posed.

"Woods. Danny Woods is my name. I own the place," he replied.

"I see. You have heard that Samantha passed away?"

Danny sighed, "Yeah. The police came by to tell me. Unfortunate."

"She had worked here for a while?"

"She was my longest serving employee. Six years she was here. When others left, she kept going. She surprised me sometimes," Danny said.

"What kind of employee was she?" Celia asked.

"She was not what you would call the model employee. She would come late every day, always had an excuse. The most common one was 'she was held up while helping a neighbor'. It got me wondering what kind of neighbors needed her help every morning. Spent too long with one customer, even when there were queues. She was good with people – great, actually. She would charm them up and keep them coming in like nobody could. She just couldn't focus very well on the big picture sometimes. Anything goes. Talking and eating while attending to customers. I mean, everyone loved her, but I kept wondering if I would have to tear up the employee code of conduct if she kept at it," Danny said.

Listening to him, it was obvious he had never really shared his perspective of Samantha with someone else.

"But you didn't tear it up for six whole years," she said.

"Oh well, you could say I learned to work with her. She was just amazing with the animals and the people. There's no doubt about it."

"Did you get along?"

Danny's eyes narrowed as he paused, as if he hadn't heard her right.

"What do you mean by did you get along? I worked with her for six years!" Danny said, clearly irritated.

"Well, it can't have been smooth sailing all the way," Celia said.

Danny stood up.

"I think it's time for you to leave, Miss Dube," he said.

"All right." Celia stood up. "Thanks for your time."

She extended her hand for a handshake, but he didn't return the favor.

As she passed the counter, the receptionist was holding a little brown puppy in her arms. It was so cute that Celia was tempted to buy it. The boys would love a little puppy.

"That's a really cute one. What breed is it?" Celia asked.

"Hey, no more questions! Please leave my premises!" Danny shouted. He was walking behind Celia.

"So, I can't be a customer now?" she asked.

"You never were. Get. Out!" Danny said, his hairy arm pointing towards the door.

Celia shrugged. She would have snuck in a question or two, or given Brenda her card at least, so Danny's continued aggression would then be somewhat justified yet needless. Then again, maybe it was good that she hadn't gotten the chance to talk to Brenda more. Judging by his reaction, Danny may have taken it out on her. Celia walked out, knowing this wasn't over by a long shot. It was obvious that Danny Woods was riled up because he was hiding something.

10

Hi Celia. So, I have 3 pimples on my face. THREE PIMPLES. The products you sold me are doing this to my face!! Never had them since I was a teen. What do I do now???

As soon as Celia had gotten into the car, she received a text notification on her phone. The message was from Mrs. Owens. Celia took a deep breath and thought quickly. Although she knew it couldn't be her products as this was the first time in a year that Mrs. Owens was giving such a complaint, there was no benefit to having her products get a bad review. Knowing Mrs. Owens, she wouldn't hesitate spreading the word about the Maven product line 'messing up faces'.

Gathering her composure, Celia texted back:

Hello Mrs. Owens! Don't worry, I have an idea of how to get that sorted. On my way.

Fortunately, there was no traffic as she headed towards the intersection that would take her to the Macan Residences. As she waited for the lights to turn green, Celia remembered that she had an organic skin cleanser that could help ease Mrs. Owens' situation. So instead of turning right, she turned left and headed to her house. She estimated she would be there in about fifteen minutes. She hoped her quick text response would buy her some time before she got to Mrs. Owens's house.

It was as Celia was waiting to turn into her driveway that she saw him. He was dressed in all black, masked slightly by the growing avocado tree right next to the door. She went into attack mode. The intruder hadn't seen her, so as she turned into her driveway, she revved her engine and sped in. He was startled, but she was only getting started. As she closed in on the intruder, she pressed her car horn and it blared furiously. Celia could now see him in her frontal view as he did the math of how soon she was going to hit him. He did look like a deer caught in the headlights. She noticed he was slender, medium height, with athletic gear that mimicked a jogger. He was probably in his mid-twenties, but had a healthy, rugged beard.

The car's wheels screeched as she braked hard, stopping just short of the intruder. He had panicked, already anticipating the crash. He jumped atop her hood and leaped off to the other side, running as fast as his track shoes could carry him.

Celia wanted to get out and run after him, but her door jammed. She made three attempts before giving up, slamming the steering wheel in frustration. She later realized she couldn't get out as she had not switched off the central locking. A safety feature she loved, but at that moment she didn't think fast enough. He was gone.

Her hands shaky, she reached for her phone and called the police.

"Tell me again what he looked like," the detective asked Celia. She had expected Detective Koloane, but she was told he was on another call. It wasn't the norm to see flashing police lights in her neighborhood, and she could see her closest neighbors peep through the curtains with curiosity.

"Like I said before, it happened so fast. Um, he was in a black tracksuit and track shoes, as if he was a jogger. Actually, I think that was the idea. He came up here posing as a jogger. But no one in this neighborhood jogs in the afternoon anyway," Celia said.

"What else did you notice?"

"He was slender. And he had a beard. He was most likely twenty-five or twenty-six years old, not older than that."

"Did he have a weapon?"

"You mean a gun? No, I didn't see one. Maybe he had a lock pick. Those are pretty sharp. Because that's what he was trying to do here."

The detective and Celia had already checked the lock, and although there were scratch marks on it, the intruder had not succeeded. Though the lock looked ordinary, it had a three-step locking system, so he was fighting a losing battle.

"Possibly. A good thing you have a reinforced door at the back, maybe that's why he was trying to pick this lock," the detective deduced.

"You know, maybe this is Samantha's killer coming after me. They are trying to see what I have, and I have nothing. Tell Detective Koloane there's no way I did it if the real killers are after me," she said. She was getting convinced that this was tied to the murder somehow.

"I wouldn't jump to conclusions just yet. He's clearly not a very sophisticated intruder, seemed unprepared. His methods match that of a gang of young hoodlums who have been staging some house break-ins in the area," the detective replied.

"But are you sure?" she muttered.

"We are investigating, and when we catch them, we will list this house as one of their targets, see what a shakedown brings. For now, I would advise you to invest in a surveillance camera system."

"Oh wow, are you serious?"

"The world is not getting any safer. Just use the tech and it might help us catch him when... I mean, if he comes back. Though I doubt he will. He's learned his lesson," the detective said as he left for his car.

Celia sat at the corner of her plush bed, thinking. She had cried a little. It had shaken her boots somewhat, despite the fact she handled it well. Beside her was the case of skin cleanser she was about to take to Mrs. Owens. Her left hand was placed on a dark blue hard case. The case, which usually stayed in her closet, belonged to Trevor. These kinds of moments were when she felt most vulnerable, and she longed for his reassuring voice, his kisses on her forehead and his firm, strong bear hug. He always made things safe again for her and the boys.

Inside the case was the gun they had bought together. She had never used it herself, for she hated guns. It was Trevor's area of expertise, so she never really thought of it. Yet today, she felt that she needed to learn how to use it. Or at least open the case and hold it in her hand. Yet, she couldn't muster the will to open the case without Trevor around.

Tears had started rolling down her cheeks again when the phone buzzed. It was Mrs. Owens.

Celia, I now have SIX PIMPLES. This is getting serious. Hurry!

For some reason, the thought of six pimples on Mrs. Owens's face made her laugh. It was lighter in nature to what had just happened, so it was suitable comic relief.

I'll be there, sweetie! I'll get you back in shape!

Celia smiled as she texted. It was time to save Mrs. Owens again.

11

"Do you realize how many things I have missed out on because of you?"

Mrs. Owens was fuming at an apologetic Celia, who had just arrived. Celia did a quick once-over of Mrs. Owens' face and found that the pimples were quite small. They were on her cheeks, where neither the eyeliner nor the lipstick would get to, so they were ruled out as the causes. If the foundation was suspect, Celia had the comfort of proving it had never affected Mrs. Owens because she had been buying it from her for almost a year. Celia was ready to challenge this.

Mrs. Owen went on, "I was due at seven in the morning to turn up at Gladwell's for a breakfast meeting. Ha, I woke up and these pimples said 'good morning' to me instead! There were two tiny ones, but by midmorning they had grown and given birth to a third one! Speaking of mid-morning, I was supposed to be taught how to play golf by Mrs. Meadows but was I there? No! Why? Because I had these three pimples who were singing 'stuck on you' lyrics to me on repeat!"

Celia sniffled a laugh without wanting to, because this was comical theater. Mrs. Owens noticed it, unfortunately.

"Celia, you think this is funny? Do you know how traumatizing it is to have wrinkles and pimples and aching bones at the same time? Well, you wouldn't know because you have neither, but sympathize with me!" Mrs. Owens ranted.

"I'm sorry, I didn't mean to play down your distress, sincerely. You know I wouldn't want anything else but the best for you. Here, let's try this right away." Celia handed Mrs. Owens the skin cleanser bottle. "Apply this around the pimples. Simply dab it on a clean pad and apply it around your face once you've washed it. It should be easing up in a few hours." "So, they will be gone today?" Mrs. Owens asked excitedly.

"No, they won't be gone today. But you will see them ease up. Be patient with your skin. However, I have to say I don't think any of my products did this," Celia asserted.

"What do you mean?"

"Have you changed your diet recently?" Celia asked.

"Not really."

"Are you sure? Nothing new from the store that you don't usually eat?"

"I mean, the only thing I haven't eaten for years was the nuts my friend brought me from Egypt," Mrs. Owens replied.

"Nuts? What nuts?" Celia asked.
 "You know, nuts. Peanuts."

"And when did you get these?"

"They came in yesterday morning. I maybe had one or two just to see what they tasted like," Mrs. Owens said. "They are pretty good, you should try some."

With that, Mrs. Owens went to the kitchen and came back with a bag of peanuts in hand.

Celia took the bag, and instead of taking a handful, read the ingredients on the pack. Moments later she said, "Yeah, I think it's possible you are allergic to these nuts. Don't take any more."

"Oh, come on now, they are top-notch," Mrs. Owens said.

"Well, then staying off them for a few days shouldn't be a problem, right?" she asked.

"What if I go somewhere during my free time and encounter nuts somewhere else? What then, huh? You are asking for the impossible."

"Tell me, what exactly do you do with your free time?"

"I go places, I already told you. In fact, I am supposed to go for a charity event tonight. That's why this pimple issue was so important to me," Mrs. Owens said.

"You are part of a charity? Which one?" Celia asked, surprised because as much as she knew of Mrs. Owens' generosity, she had never heard her being involved in a charity before.

"The Color Circle. We plant flowers at iconic sites that need a little more color and pizazz around them. Make the town livelier," she said with a smile.
Celia was genuinely fascinated. It sounded like a novel idea, yet at the same time it had the air of pretentiousness to it. Her curiosity aroused, she wanted to debunk her own assumptions.
"Tell me more. Where do you meet? Who leads it?"

"Oh, we meet at the site we intend to fix up, if it's close enough. If not, we get onto a bus and drive together to the location. No frills, just people and flowers. Oh, it was started by this charmer called Dennis Damonze. Quite the lover boy that one."

"Dennis Damonze? Isn't he married?" Celia asked, surprised by the lover boy tag.

"I wouldn't know to be honest, I'm just two trips in. But from what I have seen and heard, he likes the ladies in there, the younger ones of course, and the ladies love him."

"Interesting," Celia said. This new piece of information about Dennis was something worth looking into. "Do people of all ages come too? Because my boys love flowers."

"Oh yeah, kids come too. Although today's event might run a little late, so you might want to use your car," Mrs. Owens said.

"Can I take that as an invitation?" Celia posed.

"Oh heck, why not? I leave at five, so you better be here on time," Mrs. Owens said as she went to wash her face.

Mrs. Owens' car, followed closely by Celia's, drove into the car park of the Royal Heritage Fountain, a historical site that was over a hundred years old. It once housed a functioning fountain that was a key landmark of the town as it came up. Legend had it that travelers would often make a first stop at the fountain to have a drink and ended up settling in the area.

There was a sizeable group of people already there: men, women and a few children and teens. It was quickly obvious to Celia that the majority of the attendees were women in their thirties.

"How do I look?" Mrs. Owens asked after they had stepped out of their cars. She wore an elegant sundress and flats together with a sunhat, despite the fact the sun would be setting soon.

"You have asked me so many times," Celia said.

"Yes, but the light here is different!" Mrs. Owens replied. She was gently feeling up the pimples.

"You look fine, Mrs. Owens. The pimples are already getting smaller," Celia reassured her.

"I hope so, my dear. I hope so," she replied.

As they walked through the animated crowd, there were ushers handing out two flower seedlings to each attendee. Celia handed one each to her sons and took two for herself. It was as she was handing John his seedling that she spotted Karen Damonze. She was looking immaculate and polished, in a tweed jacket, jeans and boots. She was quite some distance from the main crowd.

However, Celia noticed that Karen was gesticulating wildly to someone who was out of Celia's line of vision. Karen was clearly agitated. Who was she having a tiff with?

"Come with me, boys," Celia said as she led her sons forward, slowly moving in a direction that would get her to see the other side of the heated argument she was witnessing.

Once her line of sight was clear, Celia got what she needed. It was a full-blown argument between Karen Damonze and her husband, the so-called lover boy, Dennis.

12

If gestures alone could kill, then Karen would have killed her husband Dennis with her animated hand movements. Although Celia couldn't hear what was being said, she could tell that Karen was livid. Dennis was trying to calm her down, but she was having none of it. Karen eventually threw up her hands and stormed off towards her car. Dennis watched her leave and shook his head. In the distance, wheels squealed as Karen drove off.

Dennis, still stumped by what just happened, turned towards Celia and their eyes locked. He realized she had seen it all. He took in a deep breath and walked towards Celia.

"Hello there. You must be one of the new arrivals," Dennis said, forcing his best smile possible. He was dressed in a cream polo shirt, blue camouflage pants, and had a sweater draped over his wide shoulders. His hair was cropped nicely, and when he smiled, it revealed his bright white teeth. Celia could feel the charm that he oozed.

"Yes, first time here," she replied.

Dennis stretched out his hand, "Dennis Damonze."

Celia shook it. He had a strong grip. "Celia Dube."

"Welcome to the Color Circle! And who are these little guys?" Dennis shook the hands of Celia's sons, who were never shy of strangers. "You have some handsome boys here to give me competition," he said with a chuckle. A charmer who was self-aware of his power, Celia mused.

"Oh, the world won't be ready for them once they turn eighteen. I hope, um, things are okay between you and...?" Celia asked.

"Yeah. Sorry about that. Karen, my wife, sometimes gets edgy. It's nothing serious, just another day in the office we call marriage. I apologize for that and hope this doesn't affect your experience here today?" Dennis seemed genuinely contrite, and Celia empathized.

"Just give her time and try to reassure her that you mean well," Celia advised. "Color Circle sounds interesting to me and the boys. How do I sign up?"

"You love flowers?" he asked.

"I do, but my boys love them more," she said with a laugh. James gave her a playful nudge and she patted him on his shoulders. "What inspired you to start this?"

"My father had a home garden. Whenever he went in to check on his flowers, I would join him. I got hooked, and I guess that's partially why I started all this," he said.

"Did someone say got hooked?" a soft voice asked.

A young woman in her late twenties with long hair appeared out of nowhere, slinking her hand through Dennis' left arm. Celia was amused, waiting for Dennis to react.

"Hello Stacy. I was just introducing Celia here to what we do," Dennis said as he gave her the once over. She was wearing a crop top and fitting jeans that accentuated her curvy figure, so Celia didn't blame him for checking her out.

"Hey Celia. It's all fun and sun at the Color Circle," Stacy said.

"I'm sure it will warm us up nicely," Celia replied as she watched Dennis. He was clearly not going to move Stacy's arm away. Celia immediately understood Karen's anger.

Later that night, after Celia and the boys had returned home and had dinner, her mother called.

"Hi Mama."

"Hello darling. How did things go today?" Mrs. Matinise asked.

"It was fairly decent. I just had to help out Mrs. Owens, who thought my products were messing up her skin. I also had a few interactions with people who were at the party," Celia said. She didn't want to let on too much about the case, but her mother was keen on it.

"Have the autopsy results been released?" Mrs. Matinise asked.

"Not yet. At least, I don't know anything from the police. I actually want them to come out. It should help get me off the suspects list quite fast," she said.

"I would think so. How are you handling it?"

"Trying to be patient. Also, it's not just about clearing my name. Samantha was full of life, and I can't shake off the question of who would want her dead."

"You are not a detective, Celia," Mrs. Matinise said.

"I know, but think with me here. Azzara, her former high school nemesis, was serving snacks at the party. Could she have done something?"

"Too obvious. I mean... why would she even try?" Mrs. Matinise posed.

"Hmm. But she had an easier way to do it, you know. The motive is maybe not strong enough. Karen Damonze, another former schoolmate, was arguing with her husband tonight because he loves women. Maybe he..."

"...had a fling with Samantha?" Mrs. Matinise finished. "You would have to prove a connection between the two of them."

"Strong motive. Then there's Melanie, who I need to find out more about. Most intriguing of all is Samantha's boss at the animal shelter, Danny Woods. A man who is just full of aggression. Although she worked for him for six years, maybe something happened that ticked him off..." Celia said.

"What on earth could that be? How could he have done anything to her at the party? He wasn't even there."

"Maybe she found out something shady about him," Celia said, her eyes widening. "That's it!" she said as she paced the room.

"What are you on about?" Mrs. Matinise asked.

"What if the person who wanted her dead was not at the party that day?"

13

The next afternoon Celia was shopping at the grocery store before picking up the boys when she spotted Detective Koloane at the cleaning detergent aisle. He was dressed down as if he was off duty. He sported a checked shirt and some jeans, a far cry from the official suit she first saw him wearing at the police station.

It had been a couple of days since he hounded her at the station, and she kept replaying the interrogation in her head to see if she had implicated herself. Each time, she concluded she had been honest about everything. The truth will always win, her mother would say. However, Celia didn't like having a target on her back.

She walked up to him.

"I hear the Supreme powder works wonders on your

clothes," Celia said. Strange conversation starter, but what the heck.

Detective Koloane turned to her and raised an eyebrow.

"Celia Dube. What a coincidence," he said as he went on scanning the shelf. "Why would you think I am looking for detergent, when there are other things on this shelf?"

"Just a guess," she replied.

"Well, that's not a good way to go," he said. He was clearly not in the mood for a chat, but Celia wanted answers.

"So, what's the latest on the autopsy?" she prodded.

"Nothing yet. Toxicology results take time to do in the case of poisoning," Detective Koloane replied.

"So, it's poisoning now? She didn't like, fall down the stairs and break her neck?" she asked.

For the first time, Detective Koloane smiled. "No broken necks. This is substances. So, it's either in the food she ate, the drinks she had, or the makeup that was applied on her," he said.

Hearing from Detective Koloane that she was still on

the list of possible suspects really brought a chill to her spine. She didn't produce the makeup. Could it contain poisonous chemicals? What if after she had left the party, the actual killer had planted the poison on her products? What then? She could feel the shelves closing in on her, and suddenly she didn't want to be there anymore.

"Thanks for the update," she said. She dropped the empty basket she was going to use and headed for the exit.

As she got to her car, her phone buzzed. It was a text from Mrs. Owens.

Hi. I didn't have any peanuts today. The pimples are still on me. What do I do now?

Celia didn't have an answer. She turned on her car and drove off fast.

As soon as she got home, Celia got down to work. She took out her pen and notepad, then laid out every product she had used at the party, as well as those she had sold to Mrs. Owens. She started checking the labels and noting down common ingredients. She was going to have to research what her products were made of, because if there was poison in there and she didn't know about it, ignorance wasn't going to be a defense.

14

"Can we do the burger run?" James asked Celia, tugging at her skirt.

"Get your brother and then we can roll out," she replied.

"Yes! Yes! Yes!" James said, as he ran off to get John.

Ever since Trevor's death, Celia had tried to make sure she would do the activities he liked doing with his sons. Going to the park, swimming, football at the beach and going out for takeout lunches or dinners.

That Saturday, the boys were craving some burgers. They always went to Big Mike's Burger Palace for those. The restaurant had been around for years. Going there wasn't just a lunch treat; she felt at ease knowing she was doing the things that would make him smile.

When they got there, James was the first to jump out

and run towards the restaurant entrance. John was a close second. Walking away from her car, Celia spotted Azzara Basson in the car park of the adjacent building. Azzara was carrying a serving tray to the back of her SUV, whose trunk was open. Celia paused and waved to her boys.

"Hey, James, John, come with me!"

"But I thought it's burger time!" James said.

"It's burger time, but I have to say hello to an old friend, so come on now," she replied.

The boys tugged along, albeit a little sluggishly as a form of protest.

"Hello Azzara!" Celia said as she got close. Azzara, who was clearly busy, looked up with a quizzical expression.

"Hi. You look familiar..." Azzara said, trying to remember.

"Celia Dube. We went to high school together. We met at Rosie's party?" she clarified.

"Oh yes! Sorry for my rude memory. Hi Celia! I would shake your hand, but well, you can see for yourself!" she said with a laugh.

Celia realized Azzara was quite personable and not as serious as she thought she would be.

"That's okay, we don't mean to interrupt," she said.

"No, no trouble at all. I was just finishing up actually," Azzara replied.

"So, you supply food here too?" Celia asked.

"Yes, they had some company breakfast meeting and asked for a few bites to keep things going. A small set up. I usually have a team with me, but they are setting up for a wedding and this is manageable for me," Azzara said.

"Oh, so you handle both individual and corporate gigs?" Celia asked.

"Yes. Mostly corporates. I make more money there, so it's my core business," Azzara said.

"Wow, good for you. I supply beauty products, so most of my clients are people. No room to do corporates, really. You're doing well."

"Thank you. Hey, every business has its niche. Anyway, if you ever have a gig or need to do an event for your clients, drop me a line. I can give you a good deal," Azzara said as she handed Celia her card.

"Thanks! I'll keep it in mind. All the best with the wedding!" Celia replied as she and the boys headed back to the restaurant.

"It's burger time!" The boys shouted as they ran towards the restaurant for a second time. A man was at the door and opened it for the boys as they got closer.

"Thank you for that," Celia said to the stranger who was still graciously holding the door open for her to get in.

"Anytime, Miss. I saw you talking to the lady at the SUV there. She's a friend of yours?" the man asked.

Celia paused, turned to him and said, "We went to the same high school. You know her?"

"Yeah, she used to supply food to a construction company I was working at two years back," he replied.

"Oh really? How was her food?" Celia asked.

"It was pretty good at first, until things went south," he replied.

"What do you mean by that?" she asked, her ears pricked up.

"One time, shortly after having her food, a lot of guys fell ill. Had to be rushed to hospital. Food poisoning, they called it. Two guys didn't make it," he said.

"Oh my, sorry to hear that. What happened after that?" Celia asked.

The man shrugged, "We never saw her again. I thought she got locked up - until I saw her today. Listen, I don't know who looks out for her and has kept her out of prison, but I wouldn't go near her food with a ten-foot pole."

15

"Does a traffic light have eyes in it?"

Celia was distracted. She was driving the boys home and John kept asking her questions about everything he could see along the way.

"Er... eye bulbs," Celia replied.

They had eaten burgers to their fill, and she uncharacteristically allowed them to have a bottle of soda each, which could be adding to the sugar rush they were having. She usually fired off answers to their inquisitive questions about everyday things without much fuss, but her mind was on overdrive. Not only was she navigating unusually heavy traffic, but she was also playing back what the man at the restaurant had said to her.

'Two guys died that day.'

'I wouldn't go near her food with a ten-foot pole.'

What he had said only proved three things; Azzara had a history of serving bad food, people had actually died from it, and she had gotten away with it. Azzara could be a cold-blooded killer who wouldn't be phased doing a number on Samantha. Could it be possible that what they thought as farfetched, a grudge from their Miss Happy Springs fallout, was true?

Celia started replaying her memories of high school. Samantha was always the happy-go-lucky one, but Celia saw another side of her when Azzara came into the picture. It had started at the lunch canteen with a war of words between the two. It got personal later that day during catwalk practice at the gym studio. The war of words turned physical, and the girls tore at each other. They had to be separated by their coach. They both had bruised faces, but Azzara was slightly worse off. People in her corner always said that if she hadn't been bruised, she would have beaten Samantha in the competition. Celia didn't see it that way. Samantha was always the more natural model, who really had a passion for it. Azzara knew she had the look and just wanted to add the win to her accolades. Passion won.

Azzara and Samantha never spoke to each other again. Until maybe Rosie's party. The idea of a long-running grudge still wasn't strong enough, Celia felt. Maybe something else had happened in recent times to revive their rivalry.

The traffic was acting up. Celia decided to turn into Bay Street and gain some time.

"Mom, why is it called a billboard?" John asked again.

"Billboard? I'm not sure. Maybe it was invented by a guy called Bill," Celia replied, knowing she was not giving her son any meaningful knowledge.

"I should invent mine. Call it a Johnboard," he mused.

The traffic on Bay Street was moving along nicely, and Celia was glad she made the decision to use it. As she drove, she spotted the familiar form of Brenda, the animal shelter receptionist, standing at the bus stop. Celia would have driven right past her if she wasn't carrying the boys, because she usually drove faster. She immediately slowed down and pulled over. She honked to get the girl's attention. Brenda came to the passenger side window and recognized Celia.

"Hey! Where are you headed?" Celia asked.

Brenda hesitated before saying, "Going towards the Baobab road."

"That's along my route. Hop in," she said, waving her in.

Brenda got in quickly, "Thanks for this."

"No problem," Celia replied. "You're off work early?"

Brenda winced at this, then said, "Yes, I took the day off. It's been a busy week,"

"I hear you. Just taking the boys back home after a lunch treat. I'm just as tired as you are, they are quite a handful," Celia said, trying to loosen her up.

Brenda attempted a smile, but it didn't come off. She nodded instead. Celia could tell there was something off, because the person she met a few days ago was warm and bubbly.

The car came to a gentle stop at the intersection of Baobab Road and Felt Road. Celia pulled over to the side, off the tarmac.

"Here we are," Celia said.

"Thanks again for the ride, I really appreciate it," Brenda said.

"You can call me Celia."

"Thank you, Celia."

"You're welcome," she replied.

Brenda got out of the car. Celia was about to drive off, but thought otherwise. She had to talk to her. She switched off the engine, put on the handbrake and got out.

"Wait for me, boys," she said as she locked the doors.

Brenda was walking slowly, her eyes on her phone.

"Brenda, wait!" Celia shouted. Brenda stopped and turned. Celia got to her quickly.

"Look, the person I met the other day was very warm and happy. You're not that person today. Are you okay?" Celia asked.

'Yeah, I'm fine, just a little tired," Brenda replied, avoiding eye contact.

"Are you sure? You can talk to me, you know," Celia offered.

That's when the dam broke. Brenda started tearing up. Celia stood by her in support.

"Tell me what's wrong, Brenda. If there's any way I can help you, I will," she reassured her.

"I... I just lost my job. I was fired today," Brenda said. Celia felt for her, and for some reason wasn't surprised. She imagined a manager like Danny Woods would be a nightmare to work with.

"I'm sorry to hear that. Why was that?"

"I usually tell the manager that he should communicate better, teach me things so I can work better. But he just expects me to walk in every day and do things, even those that I have never been trained to do. He then starts shouting at me, sometimes in front of customers, when I fail to do what he asked me to do. It was becoming a vicious cycle, and today, I had enough of his bullying and rudeness. So, I told him off and…" Brenda's voice tailed off.

"And…?" Celia whispered, putting a hand on her shoulder.

"And he fired me instead," Brenda mumbled, her voice shaky.

Celia knew about them, bosses who want you to get better at your job at the drop of a hat, but too lazy to put in the time or money to help you become the best version of yourself.

"Or maybe he wanted me to cozy up like Samantha, I don't know," Brenda added.

Celia was struck by what Brenda had just blurted out.

"What do you mean, cozy up?"

Brenda bit her lip, as if gathering the strength for the words she was about to say.

"I'm not supposed to be telling you this, but Samantha and Danny had something going on."

16

As Celia approached her driveway, she was still trying to process what Brenda had just told her.

Then she spotted a figure at her front door. Instinctively, her mind flashed back to the intruder who had tried to break in. But the person moved, and she realized it was her mother. Why was she here today? Celia wondered to herself.

Once the car was parked, the boys excitedly ran out to hug their grandmother.

"Steady now boys, steady!" Mrs. Matinise said as she laughed.

"What are you doing here, Mama?" Celia asked.

"Is that the welcome I get from you?" Mrs. Matinise asked with a frown.

"I almost thought you were the perp..." Celia caught

herself. She had never told her mother about the episode with the intruder. Mrs. Matinise's eyes furrowed a bit more.

"I lost my house keys at the market for some strange reason, never happened before, and here I am. The spare keys I gave you are still here, right?" her mother asked.

"I would never lose them. Come on in," Celia said as she walked to the door.

Once the boys had gotten over the initial excitement of having their grandma around, they retreated to watch some cartoons. Celia decided to start preparing dinner early, going for some chicken stew and rice.

"Do you want me to help you with that?" Mrs. Matinise asked.

"No mom, you are my guest today, so relax," Celia replied.

"Your choice. So, tell me more about this perp," Mrs. Matinise said. She was not one to let go of things, especially when she felt they might be bigger than her daughter was willing to admit.

Celia sighed. "First off, it's already handled. The police are investigating it and…"

"Just tell me what happened, Celia."

Celia moved closer, so that she didn't have to raise her voice. She didn't want her boys to know.

"I was just getting home the other day when I spotted an intruder at the front door. He was dressed in all black. It seemed like he was trying to pick the lock. I panicked, drove towards the door as if I wanted to hit him while blowing the car horn," she paused. "He took off."

"You are telling me all this now? Am I a joke to you?" her mother asked.

"Mama, please. Don't start. Nothing major happened," Celia said.

"So just because nothing was taken, no one was hurt, I should relax?" Mrs. Matinise asked.

"Like I said, it's being handled by the police," Celia insisted.

"I think I should stay the night now," Mrs. Matinise said.

"No need to. I don't want to scare the boys. It's most likely not related to the case. The police said there have been a series of house break-ins in the area.

The intruder won't return - my house is hard to break into," she said.

Mrs. Matinise was unconvinced. She shrugged to show her displeasure.

"So, what else do I need to know? Tell me about this case," Mrs. Matinise said. She wanted to identify any blind spots. If someone was after Celia, Mrs. Matinise wanted to be ready to point it out.

"Well, I have two possible suspects I'm trying to figure out," Celia replied.

"But that's what you had last time we spoke," Mrs. Matinise said.

"No, this is different. Funny, these leads came to me back to back. Earlier today, while I took the boys to lunch, I bumped into Azzara. She had just served some of her clients. We chatted, nothing serious. I actually didn't think much of it until, as we entered the restaurant, a man held the door open for us. He told me he knew her," Celia said.

"Was he stalking you?" Mrs. Matinise asked, concerned.

"No, Mom! Focus! He spotted me talking to her and said he used to work at this construction site where she would supply food. One time, two people died from food poisoning," Celia said.

"Wait, what? She killed them?" Mrs. Matinise said as she folded her hands across her chest.

"Allegedly Mama, add allegedly. It's a strong accusation," Celia advised.

"If that's true, why would Azzara allegedly kill Samantha?" her mother asked.

"That's what I need to figure out. They were not the best of friends in high school, you know," Celia said.

"No, Celia. There must be something bigger that happened in their adult lives that would push that dislike for each other over the edge," Mrs. Matinise said.

"You know what? I had the same thought," she said.

"She killed two people? Wow," Mrs. Matinise said, clearly was still trying to process.

"Allegedly. We still don't have a strong motive yet if she did the same to Samantha," Celia added.

"Well, people dying because of your food is a strong enough reason, no? And why is she still out on the streets, running her business?" Mrs. Matinise asked.

"That's what I would like to know. I'll dig up something on the internet once I'm done here," she said.

"What was the next thing you got?" her mother asked.

"Ah, yes. We were driving back home just now, and I saw the receptionist from the animal shelter at the bus stop. I gave her a lift. I noticed she was not quite the bubbly, lively girl I met, so I asked her what's wrong. She didn't tell me. After I dropped her off, I went after her - you know, away from the boys listening in. She broke down and told me she had just been fired."

"All right. And?"

"And, I guess because she no longer owes her boss any loyalty, she dropped a bombshell. Apparently, her boss and Samantha, who used to work there, were having a little thing."

"What do you mean a little thing?"

"A fling! Come on, work with me here!" Celia said, careful not to get too loud.

"I get what you mean, I just wanted to be sure. So they were sharing time in the sheets, huh?"

"Yes, and now my suspicions about the manager have just gone up from fifty to eighty percent," Celia said.

"I hope you are not planning to talk to him?"

"I'm considering it," Celia replied.

"You're not a detective, Celia. How about Rosie? Is she also on the list?"

"No, Rosie is Rosie. She doesn't seem to have had issues with Samantha," she said. "The only person I have not heard much about or talked to is Melanie Dawes."

"Well, if you haven't heard about her, then maybe she's not part of the mix," Mrs. Matinise said.

"Or she might be. The best killers hide in plain sight, they don't make headlines. She's a librarian, the perfect branding for someone who needs to look as harmless as a fly."

Celia paused for a moment and looked at her watch. It read four o'clock. The library closed at six in the evening. She was feeling lucky and maybe going for a trifecta of strong leads wasn't going to be a bad idea. It would give her something to chew on later in the night as she put the pieces of the puzzle together in her mind.

"You know what? Maybe you're right. We should swap roles," Celia said, taking off the apron and handing it to her mother.

"It's about time! I was wondering when you would add some seasoning to that stew."

"I already did," she replied.

"Didn't feel like it. You can smell if it's well-seasoned. You forgot my great kitchen teachings?" Mrs. Matinise asked.

"I'll enroll back in your class when I get back," Celia said as she grabbed her car keys.

"Where are you going?" Mrs. Matinise asked.

"To renew my library card," Celia said as she headed for the door.

It had been years since Celia had been in the library, and it had changed. It was still a small one in terms of size, with just one floor to its whole layout. When she would drive past it, she had a passing admiration for the new modernized architectural design that added a sharper, wedge-like feel at the corners. Now, as she stood in front of it, she truly appreciated just how good it looked.

She walked in through the sliding glass doors and

strode to the counter. It was well spaced out and quiet, like a library should be. They were using natural light and low energy bulbs for the lights, possibly to keep costs manageable. The library had shelves mapped out well across the space. Judging from the empty tables lining the center of the hallway, most of the day's readers had already left.

Standing behind the lengthy varnished wood counter was the nerdy yet smart form of Melanie Dawes. Maybe it was the glasses or her straight lips and inquisitive eyes, but Mel always looked like a genius. Celia was sure this had opened many doors for her, because Mel had grown up in a tough part of town, and for her to reinvent her destiny like this was commendable. Mel was arranging some books, which had most likely just been returned.

"Hello Mel, is it too late to renew my membership?" Celia asked.

Mel looked up, all serious. A smile broke on her face when she realized who it was.

"Celia," she said. "Well, if it wasn't some minutes to closing time, I might have considered it."

"But I think you should because it's not yet closing time," Celia countered.

"It's a bit of paperwork and it might spill over past

the official hours. I unfortunately don't get overtime here," she replied. "Can I help you in any other way?"

"Actually, you can," Celia said. "You were at Rosie's party too when Samantha died. What do you remember about that day?"

"No, I really don't want to talk about that tragic party again. The police have already been here and asked me all the questions," Mel replied and went back to arranging the books.

"But I'm not the police. It's me, Celia. We can talk as friends."

"Even worse," Mel replied, working more urgently. She picked up the books and headed down the hallway. She searched out the shelves where each book belonged. Celia followed her as she tried to charm her into a conversation. Mel was having none of it.

"Celia, you are eating into my work time," she protested.

"But there's hardly anyone here. In fact, we are talking in our normal voice pitches. See?" Celia said as she raised her voice.

"I told you I'm not talking about it. Especially if you

are here because you are a suspect," Mel replied.

That statement shocked Celia. Who was talking about her this way?

"Me? A suspect? Who told you that?'' she asked.

"My own guess," Mel said curtly. "So please leave."

"Mel, you need to talk to me, considering I gave you a makeup session at the party," Celia said. Mel just stared back at her. Celia realized this was going nowhere, and she took out her card.

"When you feel comfortable, call me. I'll buy you coffee for your troubles," Celia said as she turned.

Mel looked at the card for a few moments. Then she said: "Wait!"

Celia turned around.

"Which lipstick are you wearing?" Mel asked.

"It's the ebony black. I sell them if you want one," Celia replied.

"Um, got any free samples?" Mel enquired.

"Yeah, I actually do. There should be a set of samples in the car. Give me a minute."

As Celia walked back to her car, she smiled. If free samples were going to do the trick, then she was going to use that to get what she wanted.

17

"Wait for me at the counter as I make sure that everyone has left," Mel said.

Celia had just returned with the free samples. She found Mel had touched up her hair a little and organized her front counter desk.

"No problem," Celia replied.

Mel walked away, disappearing in between shelves as she canvassed the space. Occasionally, Celia would hear the drag of a desk or a chair, probably left out of place by some lazy user who didn't consider the place as hallowed grounds. However, Celia was fascinated by how Mel's footsteps played out. The library walls had some artwork, but neither that nor the book shelves were sufficient to bounce off the sound. Echoes rang aplenty as Mel moved around the space. Celia created her own game of trying to figure out which part of the library Mel was at, and was happy to see that her mind was sharp enough to figure it out ninety percent of the time.

"All right, we are good to go now," Mel said as she picked up her bag from the counter. Celia had seen it, but hadn't thought of looking through it; it wasn't her style to snoop around in that fashion. At least, the situation didn't really call for it. She felt she was getting closer to solving the case. Someone was going to slip up, and she would be there to pick up the pieces.

"Got the samples?" Mel asked.

"Here you go," Celia said, handing three small bottles to Mel. There were three variants of the ebony range: soft, mild and intense, with the names denoting how they varied in tone.

"Oh, this will be great! Look, I don't have a car, so do you mind giving me a ride?" Mel asked.

"Which side are you headed?"

"Actually, we could go to this restaurant not far from here. They have a happy hour with drinks at half price from five to seven. We can chat there, it's a pretty cool setting," Mel replied.

Celia hadn't pictured Mel as the type to go out for drinks, so this was an interesting discovery. Plus, she had finally convinced her to sit down and talk. The day was just getting better.

As Celia drove to the restaurant, Mel gave directions while using the car's rear-view mirror to apply lipstick. She went for the soft version first, which made her thin straight lips better accentuated. The look would work great when going for a first date where she didn't want to appear to be trying too hard.

"It looks good on you," Celia said.

"I know, right? It's not loud or brash. Just perfect," Mel agreed. "Let me also test out this intense version."

"No build up to it?" Celia joked.

"No room for middle ground in this life. It's either soft or intense, hot or cold," she replied with a smile as she went for the other sample.

Celia smiled back, although she didn't fully agree with the thought. Life was full of gray areas.

The intense version also worked on her. The nature of her lips meant the look was still strong but not too intense on the eye, Celia observed. Perfect for a formal setting or party scene.

"Your boyfriend would love that one," Celia commented.

"You've been waiting to know if I have one. Smart way of asking," Mel replied as she went on checking herself. "This is a nice one too. So I think I can go with the soft one and the intense one for sure. It's okay if I keep the other one, right?"

"Sure, they are samples after all. Do you want to buy more of those two that you like?" Celia asked, keen to make a sale.

"Um, let me hang on to the free samples for now. See how it plays out in other settings, then I will give you a call for sure," Mel said.

Celia got the feeling that Mel got by with a lot of free stuff in her life, probably to make things more bearable. Maybe librarians didn't make as much money as other professions. She would let it pass.

They arrived at the Hobo Restaurant, a little place with a strong cabin-in-the-woods feel to the exterior décor. A lot of cars were parked out front, and through the large windows Celia could tell the place was nearly filled up.

"I hope we get a place to sit," Celia said.

"Oh, we will," Mel said confidently.

She was right. Inside, there were cubicles where most of the patrons sat because they had more capacity, privacy to hide your date and plush seats. The other areas had smaller, round tables with two seats. There were a couple of round tables free, and the two women took up one of them. It had a good view of the rest of the restaurant. A waiter promptly came to their table.

"Would you like to order?" the waiter asked.

"Yeah. A vodka shot for me and some of those tasty finger foods," Mel said, signaling Celia to order.

"White wine, please. Thanks," Celia said.

"Great, I'll be with you in five minutes. I hope you enjoy the evening," the waiter replied and left.

"All drinks are at half price for two hours?" Celia asked.

"Not all drinks. Just a few chosen ones. If they were all at half price, this place would be a madhouse," Mel said with a laugh. "To answer your question, I don't have a boyfriend. At least I haven't had one in the last two weeks."

"You broke up?"

"Sort of. Let's just say he felt this town was too small

for him, and he left on his bike. It had been coming, so I was like, meh," Mel said. She clearly wasn't hung up on it.

"Sorry to hear that," Celia said.

"It happens. Some of us can't keep hold of men like Samantha could."

Celia was surprised by the statement. Was it jealousy?

"What do you mean by that?" Celia asked.

"I'm sure you know this already. Everyone does. Samantha had a way with men that kept them at her beck and call. I saw her often with different guys," Mel said.

"Where did you see them?" Celia asked, her curiosity aroused.

At this point, Mel paused as the waiter brought their drinks. It was faster service than the waiter had promised, and Celia made a mental note to buy at least one drink with cash and give him a tip.

"A lot of times, right in this place. She was never shy about it, some of the men were. But she believed in loving loudly, as if she was in charge of things and not the men she was with. Most of them had deep pockets, if you know what I mean," she said.

"How do you know it wasn't just business?" Celia asked.

Mel laughed at this. "Well, the way they doted on her? It was clear to see. You are a woman, you can tell from body language the difference between a business meeting and a meet up between lovers, right?"

"You have a keen eye," Celia said.

"I guess so. That's why I like sitting here. I can see a lot of the restaurant from here. I guess it's a bad habit from the library work," Mel said with a shy smile.

Celia appreciated Mel's self-awareness. "Is this where you saw the animal shelter manager with her?"

"Yeah. That man is always here. He's here right now," she said.

"What?" Celia whipped her head left and right. "Are you serious? I didn't see him."

"You didn't know where to look. You can't see him right now, he's masked by the cubicles. But he's here."

Celia shook her head and sipped her drink.

"There's one more man who's here that I spotted often with Samantha. You can spot him if you are keen," Mel dared Celia.

Celia started scanning the place, challenged by the spatial awareness of her company. Then she spotted a familiar form. She could tell it was him, just by the sweater draped over his shoulders.

"Is that...?"

"Yep. It's the one and only Dennis Damonze," Mel announced.

18

After having a feast of the restaurant's best finger foods, Celia decided to call it a night. Two hours had passed and Mel had opened up as the evening had grown, sharing more of her woes about love, life and career. In between their conversations, Celia kept an eye on Dennis Damonze. He wasn't doing anything unusual, just enjoying a night out with friends. He had no women with him, nor did any beauty walk up to him to say hello.

As she listened to Mel, Celia had realized this was an interesting, ambitious woman who did not want to spend the rest of her life as a librarian. Mel was a traveler at heart who needed to see the world. Celia advised her of cheap ways to do this. Mel commented that she was religiously saving every last penny she could, so in twelve months' time, she'd be waving bye-bye to Happy Springs and saying hello to the outside world. Celia also knew she had one less suspect to check off her list.

As they got up after paying the bill, Celia spotted Dennis Damonze walking towards their table. He had spotted her.

"We meet again," Dennis said as he smiled widely. He shook both their hands. "I didn't know you came here," he added.

"It's my first time, actually," Celia said, "courtesy of Melanie here."

"Ah, nice. It's a pretty popular place," he said.

"So I hear. We were just about to leave though," Celia said as she motioned Mel to take the lead towards the door.

"Could I interrupt your exit for just a moment, we need to talk," he said. He seemed concerned about something, and Celia wasn't going to pass up the opportunity for more revelations.

"I'll get the bus home. Nice catching up, Celia," Mel said.

"Thanks. Text me when you get home," she urged. Mel nodded, sneaked in a quick wink at Celia and left. Celia smiled at the cheekiness.

Dennis and Celia sat back down.

"So, I have been having a few bumps around my chin recently. Never got them before and they are making me uncomfortable," he said.

Celia was taken aback. She had hoped the talk would be about something more substantial.

Dennis angled his chin upwards, trying to show her what he meant. He didn't have a beard, but his stubble was evidence he used to have one. She couldn't see any of the bumps from where she was seated.

"You can come closer if you want, or touch it a little bit," he offered. For some reason Celia took what he said as flirtatious and wasn't sure if discouraging him now would make him shut down.

"Have you changed how you shave or something?" she asked instead, ignoring his suggestion completely.

"No, not really. The only thing I changed is the shaving cream I use. Well, it's the same brand, but they released a new variant that I bought," he replied.

"Then that could be it. How about you stop using it for the next two days and just wash with warm water after a shave?" Celia suggested.

"No lotion suggestions or something? I feel pretty plain after a shave if I don't apply something," he replied.

"Just do this for the next two days. We are trying to eliminate the possible cause. Adding another chemical to the skin might complicate things. Once you do that, I can get you something to help out with the bumps," she advised.

Dennis nodded. "Sounds good," he said. In the same moment, his hands reached for hers and he held them. It was a soft hold. His hands were amazingly warm and firm. She didn't expect this, but it felt good.

"Thank you, Celia. This has been making me very uncomfortable, but your advice is very reassuring," he said, his eyes locked on hers.

Celia found the moment a bit too intense and slowly withdrew her hands.

"I should be leaving now," she said

"Hey, it's three days to the weekend, and we'll be having another flower planting event at the St. Mathews church garden. We could meet up then. Come with five bottles of the product," he said.

"Five bottles?"

"Why not? Something tells me they are worth it," he said confidently. This made her smile.

"Five bottles it is. See you then," Celia said as she got up and walked to the door.

"See you then, Celia."

It was already dark when Celia got out of the restaurant. She figured her mother and kids must have already eaten dinner. Suddenly, Celia felt famished, even though she had eaten quite a few nibbles. Maybe it was all the talking that had transpired that was making her crave for something more. As she walked quickly to where she had parked, she couldn't see clearly in the shadowy car park. She bumped into someone else who was coming around a van.

"Sorry!" Celia instinctively said as she backed up to see who it was. To her surprise, it was Danny, the animal shelter manager. It seemed he had helped himself to one too many drinks.

"Argh, these people should put up some lights out here!" he said.

"Fancy seeing you here," Celia said. She knew he hadn't recognized her yet, and she was willing to push him along.

He squinted at her before nodding in realization.

"You're that snoopy lady. Dube," he said.

"I wasn't snooping around. I walked in through your front door," she clarified.

Danny grunted. "It's snoopy now that you're stalking me here."

"Don't be silly. I was meeting with a friend of mine," she said, slightly irritated.

Danny looked behind her, as if looking for the proof of her friend's presence.

"Seems like you are all alone to me," he said.

Celia shook her head. It was futile trying to convince this man.

"If I wasn't mistaken, I would say that's the same way you would look out for Samantha when you came to meet her here," she said.

Danny's shock was visible even in the dark.

"How did you..." he asked.

"I know things. People talk," she replied confidently.

"Brenda told you this, didn't she? It's good riddance that I fired her," he gloated.

"She's got nothing to do with this conversation. Were you seeing Samantha or not?" Celia asked.

Danny shrugged. "Yes, I was seeing her. So what?"

"Why didn't you tell me when I came over?"

"I didn't have to," he replied.

"What happened between the two of you?" Celia asked.

"We broke up the day she died. Didn't think it was important," Danny replied.

Celia wondered if that was the trigger that made him kill her.

"Where were you the day she died?"

"I was here. Drinking away my sorrows as they say," he said.

"You were here? What time exactly?" Celia prodded.

"Listen, I'm not answering any more of your questions. I'm here to have a pleasant evening, so this conversation is over," Danny said. He brushed past her and went into the restaurant.

Celia watched him walk off. In her mind, there was no doubt he may have killed Samantha. Especially if he found out about Dennis. A classic love triangle. She would love to see footage from the restaurant's security cameras. But that would have to wait till the next day, when things were a little quieter.

19

It was a sunny Saturday and Celia arrived a few minutes after four o'clock at the St. Matthew's church. It was one of the oldest churches in town, built by the first Catholics who settled in the area. Even after several retouches, it still retained its rustic feel and grandeur from the past.

She had gone back to the Hobo restaurant the day after bumping into Danny. The manager was not very welcoming to a stranger asking for their security footage, so she decided not to pursue it further - for now.

Celia headed towards the garden, which was behind the main sanctuary. There she found a buzzing crowd of about forty people talking and mingling. The crowd stood on the most pristine grass she had ever seen. It felt like a transgression that the church was allowing them to walk on their well-manicured lawn. But what stood out more was the fact that the crowd was more dressed up than they were the last time she was there. The social class of the attendees was on full display. The designer dresses, suits and fancy footwear suggested no one was there to plant any flowers. Celia tried to look out for Mrs. Owens, but she couldn't spot her.

However, she spotted Karen Damonze, who looked as elegant as ever in a designer blue dress and a matching wide-brimmed hat. She was talking to two important-looking men, probably bank managers. Karen waved at Celia, who waved back. Karen went on talking to her guests.

Celia approached a woman who stood alone, casually sipping a drink.

"Excuse me, I was wondering if this is the Color Circle event?" Celia asked.

"It sure is," the woman replied.

"Last time I was here no one was dressed up like this," Celia said.

The woman smiled knowingly. "You must be new. Out of every three monthly meet ups, two are like this. This is where the fun happens."

'When do you plant flowers when dressed up like that?"

"You don't," the woman said, pausing to take a sip. "If you go to the planting zone on the other side of the crowd, you will find other people doing it. They hire workers to plant the flowers as we do this other fun stuff. Kill two birds with one stone."

"I never expected that," Celia admitted.

"I can tell from your outfit. Don't worry, it doesn't really matter. Just enjoy yourself. It's a beautiful afternoon," the woman said.

"I intend to. Thanks for the heads up," Celia replied as she went looking for her main target, Dennis Damonze. She had the products with her and was really keen to offload the five bottles. He'd better be a man of his word.

She found him at the flower planting zone the woman had talked about. He was talking to one of the workers-for-hire. The workers were all young men and women, six in number. They were clearly people from the poorer neighborhoods who needed the gig. Celia rationalized it was better to give them a way to earn some cash than let them sleep hungry.

"Hello Dennis. Sorry to interrupt."

Dennis turned to see her.

"Hey Celia. No problem, I was just finishing up actually," he replied. He nodded at the worker, and the young man went back to work.

"Got something for me there?" he asked, as he looked at her bag inquisitively.

"I brought what you ordered," Celia said as she handed him the gift bag. Dennis received it and took out one of the bottles of cream.

"Looks fancy, I like the packaging," he said. "You know what? You were right. The bumps started reducing when I stopped using the shaving cream. Felt weird at first, but I got used to it."

"That's good," she said, happy that her advice was now working for male clients. She could now plan how to reach that segment of the market, which she had not really explored before.

Dennis took out his wallet, leafed through some notes and took out the cash.

"There you go," he said.

As she reached for the notes, he held her hand and kissed it. Celia wasn't amused, but she found it hard to withdraw her hand.

"Thank you. You are a lifesaver," he added.

Celia knew he was being dramatic, yet understood why he was such a hit with women. He knew how to connect with them on a visceral level and make them feel special without losing his power over them. Even though she was resisting his advances, she could tell that had the circumstances been different, she would have warmed up to him quite quickly. She hadn't felt that way in a long time.

"Why do you always say thank you in such dramatic ways?" she couldn't help asking.

"It comes with the territory. I suggest you get used to it," he replied with a wry smile as he walked away.

Celia shook her head. That business complete, she figured she might as well grab something to eat. She walked towards the gazebo, where the finger foods and drinks were being served. As she got close, she saw the woman she had talked to earlier.

"I see you have a fan in Dennis," the woman said as Celia was about to go past her. Celia slowed to a stop.

"Excuse me?" she asked.

"Dennis, he's a fan of yours," the woman reiterated.

"What do you mean, exactly?"

"He likes your work, so he's definitely going to be doing business with you," the woman said.

"How exactly do you know what business I do?"

"It's hard to miss out on the Maven beauty line if you like looking good," the woman replied.

"You use our products?"

"I used to. Haven't had a supplier in this area. Unless…" the woman left the statement hanging as an invitation.

Celia took out her card. "Celia Dube. Call me when you need something."

The woman took the card. "Abby Dwente. I'll be reaching out; you are a lifesaver."

Celia didn't know if Abby was a lip reader, because it was uncanny that she was using Dennis' line, yet she believed they were out of earshot.

"I'll be waiting for your call," Celia said as she walked off. Abby had a strange aura, in Celia's opinion. Was she Danny's assassin-for-hire? Why was she watching her every move? Although she realized that she might be overthinking things, Celia resolved to keep an eye on Abby for the rest of the afternoon.

The food serving area was simple, consisting of a few tables bearing a decent variety of tasty nibbles that included chicken wings, biltong, sosaties and meatballs. Celia wasn't in the mood to eat meat, so she started eyeing the confectionaries. Displayed tastefully were cupcakes, brownies and doughnuts.

"Never thought you had a sweet tooth."

Celia turned to her left and saw the smiling Karen Damonze watching her.

"Ah, I didn't feel like chowing down the meaty bites today," Celia said.

"That's a shame, seeing as Azzara has pulled all the stops to serve us today," Karen said.

"This setup is by Azzara Basson?" Celia asked.

"The one and only. She always comes through. What would I do without her?"

"Aren't you worried about...?" Celia started, but Karen cut her off with a casual wave of her hand.

"Nothing has been proven. Azzara has given me good service for years with no issues. I'm not going to ditch her now in her time of need," Karen replied.

"It makes sense," Celia said. Karen was right. There

was no evidence at present against Azzara. However, the revelation that Azzara was behind the food setup made Celia hesitate placing anything on her plate. Karen noticed her discomfort.

"You know what? I baked a cake yesterday that I wanted to present later. I'm not sure how it came out. Do you mind being my unofficial taster?"

Celia was open to new options at this point. "Sure, where is it?"

"Follow me," Karen said.

She led the way towards the chapel kitchen, which was overlooking the garden. It was a spacious kitchen with everything you would need to do a cookout, and the church seemed to have these quite often. It was clean and organized too. Celia was impressed.

"Great space, huh? We didn't use it because we already had Azzara in mind, but when I got here, I just had to use it for something," Karen said.

Karen took out a fruitcake from the oven, which was covered in foil. She had already cut it into four large quarters. She carefully cut out a thin slice from one of the large pieces and placed it on Celia's plate.

"Forgive me. I don't want to give you too large a

piece because there are forty people it needs to feed. Let me get you a fork," Karen said.

"It's fine. No need for a fork," Celia said. She had a serviette on hand for that purpose, so she saw no need to stain any cutlery. She was studying the cake slice, which looked enticing. "It looks fresh. Are those strawberries?"

"Yes, I added a few in there. I initially wanted to put in dates, but I have never tried those before. At least I have tried it with strawberries once. All right, I'm a little nervous so be gentle with your feedback," Karen said with a smile.

Celia was amused. She held the slice in her serviette and took a bite. It was soft and rich in flavor. She bit into the strawberry and loved it.

"Oh wow. You really did something with this one," Celia said.

"Okay... Is that something good or something bad?" Karen asked.

There was a pause as Celia kept chewing, keen to swallow the rest of the cake before she continued her review.

"It's good! Very nice, I love it. You know, strawberries always taste better when they are part of a cake, not when you eat them on their own. Karen, you aced it there. Let me gobble down the rest of it. Wow," Celia said as she reached for the other half.

She fumbled a bit and couldn't get a good grip of the piece. Before she could salvage the situation, the cake wrapped in serviette fell from her hands onto the kitchen floor.

"Oh, drat," Celia said as she moved to gather up her mess. As she leaned forward, she couldn't maintain her equilibrium and suddenly she was on the floor as well. She tried lifting herself but her whole body, arms and legs felt like jelly. She somehow managed to turn over and lie on her back. Everything was blurry, but she could still hear the distant sounds of people and the sound of Karen's footsteps approaching.

She saw Karen's blurry face come close to hers. Celia wanted to ask her what was going on, but her mouth could hardly move. Karen's blurry face was saying something though, and Celia forced her foggy mind to listen.

"You think you were going to come here, give my husband that silly gift in front of other people and get away with it? At our event? This is your fault!" Karen said as Celia started losing consciousness.

Celia's mind rushed to a deep, dark place. Images of her mother and her sons flashed across her mind.

Then it went dark.

20

She could hear a distant hum. Incessant, strong.

Then it got stronger, and stronger, until it was no longer a hum, but a beep. The persistent, regular beeping sound of a machine.

Her eyelids were as heavy as lead, but she summoned the little strength she had and managed to lift an eyelid. It took the whole of her being to raise the other eyelid, and Celia was finally able to see her mother, Mrs. Owens, and surprisingly, Rosie. The three were standing at her bedside.

"She's awake now," Mrs. Matinise said. A sigh of relief was palpable in the room.

"Where am I?" Celia asked in a weak voice.

"You are at the hospital, sweetie," Mrs. Matinise replied softly.

Celia looked around the room. The white and blue walls stared back at her. The consistent beep was from the cardiac monitor next to her bed. She watched the waves on its screen for a moment, then noticed the cables on her left arm.

"Why... what happened?" Celia asked. Her thoughts were in a jumble.

"Karen tried to get to you," Rosie said. "She... she gave you some of that poisoned cake," she added.

Suddenly the memories came flooding back; the cake, the serviette, losing her balance and Karen's blurry, evil smile.

"Oh my God, how did I survive that?"

"You had a guardian angel. Mrs. Owens was keeping an eye out," Mrs. Matinise said. "You didn't want to do it yourself, so I asked for a little help. Thank goodness she noticed you and Karen going into the kitchen. When she heard the commotion as you fell down, she came in and fought off Karen. The standby paramedics got to you in good time."

Celia turned her gaze to Mrs. Owens.

"Wow. I... I had looked for you, Mrs. Owens," she said.

"Guardian angels don't need to be seen, Celia. I had my eye on you, that's what matters," Mrs. Owens replied.

"What happened to Karen?" Celia asked.

"She was arrested immediately. She's at the station, set to appear in court tomorrow," Rosie said.

"Wait. How long have I been..."

"You've been unconscious for five days. It's been a long wait, but the doctor said it was only a matter of time before you came back to us. Don't worry, you'll be fine, no major damage. They caught it before it could mess you up. Good thing you didn't eat the whole slice," Rosie said.

Celia was grateful too that the cake had slipped from her fingers. Funny how mistakes can turn out to be blessings.

"But why? Why did she do it?" Celia said.

Rosie, Mrs. Matinise and Mrs. Owens looked at each other, as if wondering who should spill the beans.

"Okay, I'll do it," Rosie volunteered. "First of all, Karen is a crazy woman. Do you know she wanted to beat up Mrs. Owens when she came to save you?"

"Oh, she tried but she was not going to take me down. I know how to smack you with a pan real good if I need to," Mrs. Owens said with an air of defiance.

"You two fought?" Celia asked.

"I didn't hit her with the pan, I almost did though. You don't play games with me. She pushed me off you when I was checking if you were okay or not," Mrs. Owens replied.

"Before things got too crazy, we had heard the noise and came running to the kitchen. Four of us held Karen back as she shouted all sorts of craziness. Thank God the police arrived shortly afterwards. We might have been forced to mess her up a bit," Rosie added.

"But you're still not telling me why she did this? And is this how she killed Samantha?" Celia asked.

"Same poison, different snack. You're just lucky you got a little dose of it," Rose said. "Apparently, Karen and Dennis have tried to have a baby for years, but that became more complicated when she found out about Dennis' cheating. They argued all the time, but funny enough, she didn't leave him. She couldn't take it that Dennis was spending time with other women instead of getting her pregnant. Eventually Karen snapped, and decided to kill his mistresses, one by one. She planned to kill off Samantha first, and unfortunately…"

"…she saw her chance at your party," Celia said weakly.

"Exactly. You've been unconscious this long and your brain is still in detective mode," Rosie said.

Celia smiled.

Rosie continued: "Anyway, she went to Azzara's food table and took some bites, which she poisoned. When Samantha went to get something to eat, Karen intercepted her and gave her the bites, acting like the 'considerate friend'. Once Samantha devoured them all, she didn't stand a chance."

Celia remembered how Samantha had come to have her makeup done, biting into the food. If only she had known. Celia closed her eyes. The memory pained her.

"Life is just too short. Too short," Celia whispered. Her mother reached for her and squeezed her hand.

"You're still here. You're beating this, okay?" Mrs. Matinise said.

Celia opened her eyes and nodded. Her eyes welled up with tears. Keen to lighten things up, Mrs. Owens stepped forward.

"Hey, I got something for you, Celia," she said.

Mrs. Owens took out a check and showed it to Celia.

"What's this?" Celia asked.

"I'm settling all the dues I owe you for the past year. Let's start on a clean slate when you get out," Mrs. Owens said with a smile.

Celia smiled and nodded slowly.

"I also have a debt I need to repay," a voice said.

They turned their heads to see Detective Koloane standing at the foot of the bed. He had just arrived, holding a small bouquet of roses.

"Are you here to interrogate me?" Celia asked.

"I see you still have a sense of humor. Good to see you awake. Do you accept my flowers as a peace offering?" the detective asked. The bouquet was not a big one, and the flowers could be mistaken for a bunch he stole from the hospital flowerbed, but the intention was what counted.

"Sure. As soon as you confirm to my guests here that I'm no longer a suspect," she said.

"I can confirm you are no longer a suspect, Celia.

What you did, putting yourself in harm's way, was very brave, but you should have come to me with any suspicions you had," Detective Koloane replied.

"That's my girl. It runs in the family," Mrs. Matinise said.

"It sure does, Mama," Celia affirmed.

"When you get out of here, we are going to have a party," Rosie said.

"Not on my watch, Rosie. Last time..." Mrs. Matinise was discouraged from finishing her statement when Celia gripped her hand.

"Ssssh! Now what we won't do is hang on to the past. That's already taken Karen's life sideways. I wouldn't want that to happen to anyone here," Celia said.

"That sleep made you real wise, huh?" Mrs. Matinise said.

Celia smiled. "When will I see my boys?"

"An hour from now. I hope you are ready," her mother said.

"I've had five days to get ready," she said.

"Good. Focus on those boys, no more snooping around," her mother said.

Celia turned to her with a cheeky smile.

"Sorry, I have a clean slate. If there's another challenge for me, bring it on! I'm ready."

The End

Afterword

Thank you for reading Makeup and Mayhem! I really hope you enjoyed reading it as much as I had writing it!

If you have a minute, please consider leaving a review on Amazon or the retailer where you got it.

Many thanks in advance for your support!

EYEBROWS AND EVIL LOOKS CHAPTER 1 SNEAK PEEK

Celia Dube was not having the best morning.

It was one of those rare cloudy days in the suburban town of Sunshine Cove, and along with it came a chill, swept in by the cold winds from the nearby ocean.

Such dull weather was preferable to rain. Her work as a beauty consultant and makeup distributor meant that she was often driving to meet new and old clients. The rain would have made this more difficult, especially when she was trying to finish the day's work and run home to her two little sons.

The cloudy weather was not the reason she was having a difficult morning. She was seated in the large living room of one of her clients, Flavia Swane. Flavia was pacing around the room in anger. She spoke very animatedly, her afro shock of hair dancing as she protested.

"Here I was thinking that we were good friends! After eight months of throwing my money at you, can't I get even a tube of that special edition you released last month as a surprise?" Flavia exclaimed.

As Celia listened, she reflected briefly on her twelve-year-long career. She often turned to her training and experience to find solutions for such situations. Always the optimist, she had quickly learned early in her career the importance of managing client expectations. She was a great marketer, but her client base grew at a slow pace due to high competition when she started. Things changed when her husband, Trevor, died, and she knew she had to improve. Her two sons needed her and she could not let them down. So, she focused on developing her listening skills extensively, as well as taking several body language classes to learn how to read people better.

Applying these skills had made her successful. Many clients often shared positive words such as 'Celia, you understand me' or 'Celia, you are such a good listener!' which always gave her the encouragement to keep going. She was now earning a good living from a loyal client base that she enjoyed serving. For her, this job was more than selling products. It was a calling to make the people she connected with feel and look better.

"Celia, just one tube to surprise me a little. Was that so difficult to do?" Flavia asked.

Celia kept listening. She needed to be patient and only speak when the time was right. Interestingly enough, Celia was not a fan of surprises, so she tried as much as she could to avoid surprising her clients. Her husband Trevor had been the opposite. He lived for surprises, perhaps because his military training espoused its benefits. It was little wonder that her sons loved surprises too, but maybe that was purely down to childish wonder. She didn't mind the glee it brought to their faces when she got them goodie bags without notice. Surprises had their heartwarming perks.

While Celia listened to her client's complaint, she reflected on their relationship. She remembered that she had already given Flavia four freebies in recent months, the most she had offered any of her clients. Giving her a new one with this delivery of shampoo had never been on the cards. When it came to her clients, Celia walked the fine line between managing their expectations while putting them up on a mini-pedestal. She would always tell them in advance when she was running an offer on a beauty product she delivered, and what they would get in the deal. This way, when she showed up at their doors, she had exactly what they wanted. Some of them became fickle and wanted to change the nature of the 'gift' they were getting. While Celia sometimes kept options for this scenario, it wasn't always possible. In those instances, she either withheld it altogether or asked them to give it to a loved one who may appreciate it.

Flavia, needing to pause for a moment, stopped her

rant with a big sigh. Celia saw her chance to respond.

"I am sorry about this, Flavia," Celia said politely, "Bear with me on this one, especially since I have been quite generous the last couple of months. My memory is still very fresh. I remember how you danced around this very living room two months ago after I got you the gift hamper," Celia said.

Flavia paused for a moment, recollecting the memory.

"Yes, I appreciate that. But it was two months ago, my dear. Two months!" Flavia insisted.

Celia sighed. It was like talking to one of her sons about why eating junk food every day was not healthy.

"You know that as much as I appreciate your business, I can't do special offers with every delivery. So kindly bear with me for now. I will tell you this: there will be a surprise for you next month. Guaranteed!"

"It better be the special edition, my dear."

'It will not be the special edition. That's a mainline product,' Celia said to herself.

"I have a few samples of a new eyeliner that's being

introduced to the market. Would you like to be one of the first ones to get it?" Celia asked.

Flavia mellowed instantly.

"Why, yes! The last one I bought from another supplier was just horrible. It couldn't last a day! I walked around looking like an egg because I had no eyebrows! So please, bring it!" Flavia replied.

This made Celia smile.

"Consider it done," Celia said.

"You know what? I'm sorry for putting you on the spot earlier," Flavia apologized, putting both hands to her cheeks, "I appreciate the way you have explained things to me. Not many have your patience."

Celia was pleased with herself. "The pleasure is all mine. Can we conclude the deal now?"

She needn't have asked, because Flavia was already fishing through her gold-colored purse. Her long-manicured nails emerged with forty dollars, which she handed to Celia.

"As always, thanks for your business, Flavia," Celia said as she got up to leave.

"I'm sorry I was so caught up in the moment I forgot to offer you something to drink. Will you have coffee, tea?" Flavia offered. It was amazing to watch the shift from angry client to courteous client, and this satisfied Celia more than any beverage could.

"No thanks. Let's push it to my next visit," Celia replied as she headed for the door.

When she got outside, she looked up to the sky and saw a sliver of sunlight peeking through the clouds. She smiled, relieved to have served her last client, and to see the sun still shining beyond the clouds. She got into her Subaru station wagon, keen to get home to her kids.

As Celia walked towards her front door, she could hear the wild cheers of her two sons coming from within. Walking in, she was greeted by a sight that had become all too familiar the last couple of days.

John and James were standing in front of the wall-mounted wide screen television with game pads in each hand. They were playing a car racing video game, and the noise she was hearing was of them chiding each other's driving styles. They hardly noticed her arrival.

"You need to slow down to win," nine-year-old James told his younger brother.

"But you keep blocking me! We have to play another one!" James replied.

"No, we said, the winner is the winner," James said.

"You were cheating. We go again!" John insisted.

This descended into a shouting match, soon broken by Celia's shrill voice.

"All right, that's enough now!"

The two boys stopped, then ran to her, "Mom!"

They both embraced her hugging her so tight she thought she would lose her balance.

"Ease up, little fellas. I know why you're showering me with all this love," Celia said.

The two boys stepped back.

"Where's your grandmother?"

"Here as usual!" a voice said as the approaching figure of Audrey Matinise, Celia's mother, emerged from the kitchen. She wore a colorful apron and held a kitchen towel, "Welcome home, sweetheart."

"Hi, Mom. How's it going?" Celia asked as she placed her bags down and took off her long coat.

"Pretty good. We had a good time today, didn't we young men?" Audrey asked.

"Yes, grandma!" the boys replied in unison.

"It looks like they are having a little too much fun, actually. How long have they been playing this video game?"

"Maybe an hour or so," Audrey replied.

"Have you done your homework, boys?" Celia asked. The two boys looked at each other but kept silent.

"Alright, that's it. We are going..." Celia started, but her mother interrupted.

"Let them play just for tonight, okay? I will have them in check from tomorrow. Come over, I need some help with the food."

Celia paused and caved in to the idea.

"All right, you can play for thirty more minutes," she told the boys.

"Yay!" The boys cheered as they ran back to their gaming positions. Soon, they had started a new race.

"You spoil them too much," Celia said with a sigh.

"That's what grandmas are for! I'm the good cop, you're the bad cop. The boys need both," her mother replied with a cheeky grin.

Celia followed her to the kitchen where they spent the next forty minutes preparing lunch, which they ate together.

Afterwards the boys played in the backyard, enjoying the afternoon sun. Celia watched them from the living room while sipping a glass of warm water. Audrey walked up to her.

"Relax, sweet thing. It's the holidays. Let them loosen up and explore."

"But they explore the TV screen more than the outdoors these days. I need to find something new for them to do," Celia said.

Her mother laughed.

"They read for nine months a year, they have got to have some time to do other things in between," she replied.

It was at this point that an idea crossed Celia's mind.

"You know what? I know what to do," she said as she stood up to leave.

"Where are you going?" her mother asked.

"To see a friend of mine. I have just discovered a new activity for the boys," Celia replied with a wink.

The local community library looked immaculate in the afternoon sun. Since its refurbishment from the old drab exterior, it had become an aesthetic wonder around Sunshine Cove. On sunny days, its snazzy facade bounced off rays with its marbled walls and tall window panels. It had quickly become a cool haunt for young people. They would come and read from the wide array of books, or sometimes sit on the library grounds' benches under the shade of trees.

Celia walked into the library, which was deathly quiet, her footsteps echoing across the large expanse of the room. She arrived at the reception counter. A young man stood there, book in hand. He was waiting for the librarian who was nowhere to be seen. They didn't have to wait long. Another set of footsteps could be heard approaching them from behind the shelves. Melanie Dawes, donning a casual suit with her curly dark brown hair pulled into a ponytail, soon emerged.

Melanie didn't voice any greeting, smiling and nodding at them instead as she went round to the other side of the counter. Her commitment to maintain silence was impressive.

She took the young man's book, scribbled an entry into her record book, before handing it back to him. The man mouthed a silent 'thank you' and went on his way. Celia eased into his place.

With Celia, Melanie was open to breaking the rules.

"Hey, Celia. What did we say about unannounced visits?" Melanie whispered. She was genuinely happy to see her. She had few friends, and the last time she had met Celia was three weeks ago.

"That I have a special pass?" Celia whispered back in jest, "How's your day going?"

"Good, so far. Busy. The visitor numbers have been growing since we refurbished the place. It's becoming a space for human connection again," Melanie replied.

"That's great! I wanted to check in on you, and I'm glad the vibes are good. So, I remember you told me there's a kids section, right?"

"Yes, a good one. And we just added a new collection of books. You want to see it?"

"Yeah, of course. Will it take long?" Celia asked.

"Not at all," Melanie said as she walked out from behind the counter.

Just then, two people approached them from the main door. The two friends turned to look. Celia was unable to make out who it was. Melanie recognized them.

"Actually, it might take a little longer...," she said.

"Hello, Melanie!" the woman said, her voice projecting across the whole space. She was clearly not aware of where she was, or didn't care.

Melanie waved with a pained smile.

"Hello, Rachel Sablay, how are you?" Melanie whispered in response, keen to impose her rules.

Rachel wore a puzzled look on her face. "Why are you whispering?" she asked.

"We're in a library. It's standard practice," she whispered.

"Ooooh, sorry honey!" Rachel whispered back, as if surprised at the news. "I hope that won't be the case during my event?"

"It won't be. The space will be all yours," Melanie replied.

"Great! This is my assistant, Joshua. He's here to keep notes about the things we agree on. You can take me around the place?"

"Sure, let me get my notebook as well," Melanie said, turning back to the counter to pick a small notebook and pen. As she walked past Celia, she raised her eyebrows in that 'here we go' way.

Celia didn't have to be told twice. She followed Melanie; despite the fact she had no idea what was going on.

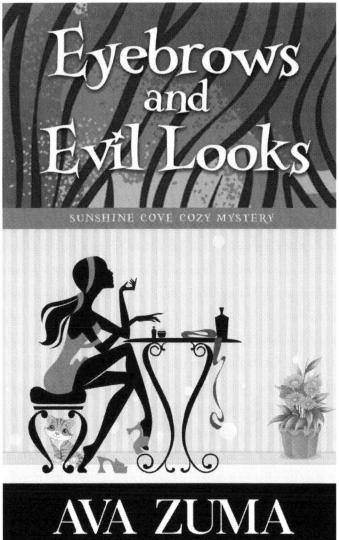

Eyebrows and Evil Looks

SUNSHINE COVE COZY MYSTERY

AVA ZUMA

ALSO BY AVA ZUMA

The Sunny Cove Cozy Mystery Series

Makeup and Mayhem (Book 1)

Eyebrows and Evil Looks (Book 2)

Nails and Nightmare (Book 3)

Printed in Great Britain
by Amazon